VOLUME FOUR

EVERNIGHT PUBLISHING ®

www.evernightpublishing.com

Copyright© 2025

ISBN: 978-0-3695-1291-8

Cover Artist: Jay Aheer

Editor: Lisa Petrocelli

VOLUME FOUR

Monsters of New York is a sizzling paranormal romance series where passion collides with danger in the heart of the city that never sleeps. Each book introduces a new, irresistible shifter—each with its own dark secrets and primal desires. From wolves and bears to elusive creatures lurking in the shadows, these powerful beings navigate love, loyalty, and mystery in a world filled with human and supernatural monsters.

Set against the backdrop of New York's vibrant streets and hidden corners, every romance is an unforgettable journey where forbidden love and heated encounters could be the death of them—or the one thing that saves them. With danger always just around the corner, the shifters must face not only the threats of their own kind but the intense pull of a love that could change everything.

Uncover the secrets, feel the heat, and discover if love can tame the wildest beasts in Monsters of New York.

VOLUME FOUR

THE LION'S RELUCTANT MATE

Monsters of New York

Elyzabeth M. VaLey

Copyright © 2025

Chapter One

Alice hesitated at the entrance to the gin bar. Unlike other bars in the area, this one didn't have a flashy neon sign advertising what it was. Instead, embossed in fancy gold letters and lit by a soft yellow glow, the words, THE GIN ROOM, invited the customer inside. The glass windows at either side allowed a distorted glimpse into the interior. She couldn't tell if the venue was packed or empty.

Hannah, from whom she'd heard about the place, had sworn that on a Thursday evening it tended to be a light crowd, especially if they had just opened. She'd told her it was the place to go to if she wanted to unwind after a hard day at work, and practice being around others. The

Gin Room is on the high end of the spectrum and has the best gin variety in town at reasonable prices. You can't ask for more.

Taking a deep breath, Alice opened the door. She was greeted with soft jazzy music playing in the background and the scent of sandalwood. She looked around. The place was empty except for the bartender behind the counter and the waiter lighting the candles on the low round tables, each surrounded by burgundy velvet chairs.

For an instant, she wished she hadn't come alone, but she shook the thought away. This was why she was here. Her therapist had told her she had to go alone to places and try to enjoy the moment, regardless of people around her. While she was there, she could read a book or take some notes on her feelings, but she had to stay for at least thirty minutes.

Swallowing hard, she approached the counter and took a seat at one of the stools.

"Gin and tonic, please," she said. How many times had she rehearsed what she was going to say?

"Welcome to The Gin Room." The waiter, a tall lanky guy dressed in a white shirt with a black vest flashed a grin at her, the light hit the flashy earring on his lower lip. "Any specific gin? We've got Bombay, Tanqueray, Beefeater—"

"Um, the pink one?" she interrupted him before she became overwhelmed with the options.

"Pink one it is. Gordon's okay?"

"Yes."

He nodded, turned his back on her, and set about getting the beverage. She let out a sigh of relief. She was sure her therapist wouldn't be pleased about the fact she'd come at the least busy moment, but hey, she was here. Right? Surely, that had to count for something. She clasped her hands together to stop from tapping on the counter.

Suddenly, the door banged open. She turned her head, and her jaw dropped. A man, well over six-feet tall stood at the entrance, two giggling girls at his side, hanging onto each arm. Alice blinked. She was stunned by the lack of clothing on the women, which was in no way appropriate for a place like this, but she was more stunned by the man ushering them silent with a gaze. He was handsome. Well-built but not in a brawny way, he wore what she had no doubt was an expensive perfectly tailored suit. His hair was on the longer side, reaching below his shoulders in reddish-brown salt-pepper waves. He walked into the venue as if the place belonged to him, his presence seeming to take over the space and squeezing the air out of her lungs as if he were physically holding her.

His gaze fell on her. She hurried to look away, her cheeks burning with shame. The unwelcome yet familiar ball of anxiety began to form in her belly. This was why she didn't go to places alone. People saw her and she didn't want to be seen. She wanted to be invisible. Thankfully at that moment the bartender came back with her drink.

He must have noticed something in her expression because he gave her another goofy grin.

"That's Axel Sala, he is part owner of the bar, which is why he can come in here with whomever he pleases." He leaned forward and lowered his voice. "If it were up to me, I wouldn't allow this display, but he's the boss. In any case, don't worry about him because he has a booth and his office at the back, so he won't bother you. He's discreet."

He winked at her, and she managed to make a noncommittal noise at the back of her throat in response.

Seemingly satisfied, the waiter walked away. Alice sighed. Her therapist wouldn't approve. Her voice rang in her head, similar to the voice of her conscience.

You had the chance to start a conversation. Why didn't you take it?

And say what? Axel Sala was a hunk? That she agreed about the women? That she wished she had the confidence to be one of them? Ugh. She glanced back to where he'd stood. He was gone, which was a good thing. Right?

She picked up the glass and took a sip. Some of it spilled down her chin onto her shirt, making her realize her hands were shaking.

"Fuck." She sat it down and dabbed at her chest with a napkin. "Easy now," she murmured.

She shut her eyes and attempted to take slow deep breaths, but the image of Axel kept dancing at the edge of her consciousness. She absently wondered what color his eyes were. Blue? Brownish like his hair? She couldn't quite tell where she was sitting, but the word "fiery" kept popping into her brain. No one had eyes like flames, though, unless… She bit her lip, opened her eyes, and hurriedly took another shaky sip of her drink. Unless they were a shifter. She rubbed the groove on the counter. Shifters.

They'd recently come out into the light and apparently had been among them forever, but she didn't know any and wasn't sure she wanted to.

There were rumors. Hundreds. Thousands. They were beastly, beyond humanity. They hunted people down. She tried to ignore them, and one couldn't help but wonder if there was some credence to it all.

If Axel were a shifter, she wouldn't be surprised. He was too tall and too good looking for a normal human being. He was the kind of guy who would never see her, the kind who would bully her—like the ones in school and college. Her heart picked up its pace and she groaned. She was supposed to be writing, working on her social anxiety, not musing about some stranger with two dollops at his side and remembering the past.

"Enough," she scolded herself. "This is the present. Stay here."

She reached into her bag and pulled out her notebook and pen. Opening it onto a blank page, she began to write.

VOLUME FOUR

Chapter Two

Axel watched her from the back, trying to ignore the dumb bimbos he'd brought with him for entertainment. Granted, they hadn't been annoying when he'd picked them up, but now that *she* was here, everything else had lost its luster. It was interesting because at his age he'd never imagined he'd meet her, and yet there was no doubt. The animal within him was as clear as daylight. It was her. His mate.

He snorted. What was he going to do with a mate? Especially one who seemed to be afraid of her own shadow, if the way her heartbeat was any indication. His proclivities were gray at best, and she seemed, well, innocent, naive, like a recently picked puppy from a litter. Curious, but terribly afraid. He would have to show her there was nothing to be afraid of. Not him. Not the world. He would have to teach her what he liked. What if she didn't like it? The unwelcome thought entered his mind, and he snarled. That was not an option. He was too old for change.

Axel took her in. At another time in his life, he wouldn't have given her a second glance. She was pretty but she wasn't exuberant. Sweet. The look of a good girl. His heart skipped a beat. His cock throbbed. Fuck. He was just looking at her and already diving into the fantasy. When was the last time that had happened?

How would she feel about being his good girl? Would she let him strip not only her clothes but also her layers of pent-up emotions, digging deep until he reached the bone? He could fully make her his, and free her from the constraints that held her back. He clenched his fists. His heart beat in his chest like never before. Excitement coursed through him. The idea of making her his thrilled him as much as if he were about to go hunting. He smiled. Then again, wasn't that what he was going to do? Hunt her. Catch her and eat her up.

He cocked his head. She was writing furiously in a notebook. Was she a writer? He could play with a writer, they tended to have active imaginations but were also a bit insecure. She didn't seem like a writer, though. She was wearing office attire. Pantsuit, conservative blazer, and a white shirt. Her hair was in a ponytail and her reading glasses kept slipping down her nose.

"Axel, join us," he heard one of the bimbos call out to him.

He turned around and surveyed them. He had chosen them for their looks. Young. Skimpily dressed. Tiny waists. Big tits. Not too bright. He shook his head and glanced back at his prey. She was so different. Yes, she was young, but her physique was not what he normally chose. She was well-endowed but nothing extraordinary. Except for the perfectly plump and ample curves. His cock twitched as the image of him pummeling into her and holding her from those love handles entered his mind.

He sighed contentedly. He was screwed, and he'd never welcomed something as much as he looked forward to this. He took a step forward. He was never the man to say no to a challenge. It was time to act.

Chapter Three

Alice scribbled into her notebook. She had successfully managed to do what her therapist ordered. She was sitting at a bar. Check. She had spoken to the waiter and ordered a drink. Check. She had made eye contact with that man she couldn't get out of her mind. Bonus check. She had sat here writing and sipping her drink, alone, for at least thirty minutes. Check.

She glanced at her smartwatch and cursed. Damn thing had run out of battery earlier in the day. She rummaged in her purse for her phone. Fifteen minutes? It had only been fifteen minutes. How was that possible? She glanced at her drink. It was almost empty. She rubbed her temples. Okay. She could do this. She could sit here alone for another quarter-hour. No one was looking at her. Heck, the place was practically empty except for a few people. This wasn't their busiest time. She was safe. She wasn't being paid attention to. She was just another customer enjoying a drink. Another person in the multitude. So why did she feel as if someone was staring at her?

"It's your anxiety." Ugh, she could hear her psychologist lecturing her—*"People are too busy minding their own business to worry about you."*

Okay. She could do this.

She set an alarm on her phone and stuffed it back in her purse. Fifteen more minutes.

She glanced at her notebook and frowned. She had mentioned him. Repeatedly. Which meant her therapist was going to ask her about it. Her cheeks burned. She didn't want to talk about him. It had been a brief glimpse. A moment her heart had fluttered. He wasn't her type. She didn't have a type. But if she did, it wouldn't be him. He was too big, too dominant. He'd eat her up and swallow her whole. She picked up her pen. Nope. She preferred to let it remain a fantasy.

"What are you writing?"

She jumped in her chair. She dropped her pen, but large hands grabbed it before it hit the ground and placed it back on the counter. Slowly, she turned around. Her heart picked up its rhythm.

He was here.

Her mouth dried. She frantically searched her brain for something to say but words eluded her. Why was he standing so close? His perfume wafted up her nose. Woodsy, yet spicy. She found his gaze. She had been right in describing his eyes as fiery. They were the color of molten amber, not brown or green, but a warm mix which reflected the light and gave the impression of being molten fire.

"Are you okay? I didn't mean to scare you."

Had his voice lowered? It echoed within her, developing an ache which spread across her chest. She tore her gaze away—which was a mistake. They landed on his lips, framed by a carefully groomed beard. They stood out like a cherry atop a decadent piece of cake.

"Look at me, Baby Girl."

Her gaze lifted back to his eyes as her brain processed what he'd called her.

"I'm not your Baby Girl," she managed to say. The words came out in a whisper so low she didn't think he could have possibly heard her.

"Not yet, you're not." He grinned. And the sight made something within her snap. Desire flushed her skin, and a tremble coursed through her.

"Please," she murmured.

He took a step closer. He wasn't touching her but he didn't need to. She could feel herself moistening, her nipples hardening beneath her shirt.

"Please what, Baby Girl?"

"Please, step." She wanted to gesture with her hand, but her fingers were glued to her sides.

"Closer?"

He took another miniscule step. He didn't have much room after all. His body bumped against her knee sending an electric shock through her. A growl-like sound came from somewhere. Whether it was him or her she couldn't say.

"Back" she murmured.

"What's your name, Baby Girl?" He touched her knee.

She shook her head. It was too much. He was too close. What did he want from her? A man like him would never notice someone like her. Anxiety came spiraling in, creating a tight knot in her stomach. Nausea assaulted her. She was going to be sick.

He must have noticed because this time he did take a small step back.

"Breathe," he demanded. "Through your nose, and exhale through your mouth. Slowly. That's it."

He gently grasped her hand and placed it on the counter.

"I am here. My hand on top of yours. Warm. You are touching the counter. Do you feel the wood? The small indentations? The stickiness? Ew…"

She chuckled. Tears prickled her eyes.

"That's it, Baby Girl."

"My name is Alice."

VOLUME FOUR

Chapter Four

The animal within him jumped for joy. *Alice.* He had gotten a name. It had almost cost her a panic attack but there had been progress. When he approached the girl, *Alice,* he thought it would be a piece of cake. He hadn't considered this vulnerability, this total fear. His protective instincts had flared even as his libido had awoken.

If there had been any doubt she was his mate, it had

dissipated as soon as he approached her. His whole being sang like a violin string at the proximity of her, and he could sense it was mutual. Perhaps that was what had triggered her reaction. He took a quick glance at her notebook. No. By the words scribbled, there was more. It wouldn't be difficult to seduce her, the difficulty would lie in gaining her love and affection. It would be a slow process, one he hadn't savored in a long time. One he hadn't realized he yearned for until now. Until Alice.

"I'm Axel."

She nodded. "Nice to meet you, I guess."

"It's a pleasure to meet you, Alice." He sat down on the stool next to hers but didn't remove his hand. He was dying to entwine their fingers together, but he had to act slowly, or he'd spook her again.

"What are you doing here by yourself?"

"Um, writing. Having a drink. What happened to your companions?"

Her cheeks flushed as she seemed to realize the inappropriateness of her question. "I'm sorry, I didn't mean to be rude. It's none of my business."

"It's a fair question. They are in the back entertaining themselves. They don't need me. They just wanted to come into the bar."

"Oh."

"How old are you?"

"Twenty-two."

He smiled.

"Baby Girl."

"I'm not a baby," she protested.

"You are to me. I'm forty."

"You don't look—" Her cheeks reddened.

"A day over forty," he chuckled. "Lying doesn't become you. I know you can see the gray in this light."

"You still look young."

Axel laughed. He debated what his next move should be. Be brazen and hope for the best, or wait to see if she said something? She seemed to be at a loss for words, hastily taking a sip from her almost empty glass.

"Would you like to go somewhere with better lighting to see them?"

Her eyes widened and she hastened to remove her hand from under his.

Too fast.

At that moment, something in her purse started to vibrate and jingle.

"I'm sorry. No. I must go. I … um, it was nice meeting you." She scrambled out of her seat and hurried to grab her belongings. "Thank you for—"

"Give me your number."

"I'm sorry, no. I'm not that type of … um … person. I need to go," she repeated.

"Alice."

She paused briefly and glanced at him. Her cheeks flushed red. Her pulse beat frantically in her neck. Axel pressed his lips together. He had to let her leave, didn't he?

"Bye."

She almost ran out of the bar. He watched her leave, slightly stupefied at his inability to keep her with him. What was he going to do now? He ran his fingers through his hair and glanced at the empty stool next to him. His gaze fell on the floor. A smile flitted across his lips. He bent over and picked up the notebook. In her haste she must have dropped it on the floor instead of into her bag. Now, if she was the type of girl he suspected, she would have written her address somewhere. He flipped the pages to the front. Bingo. Name and address. He grinned. His Baby Girl was not escaping him anytime soon.

VOLUME FOUR

Chapter Five

Alice didn't run, but she walked fast. Her heart was beating a mile a minute in her chest, and she couldn't get rid of the desire coursing through her. She'd never wanted to fuck someone as much as she wanted that man. What was with her? She wasn't that type of person. She didn't go weak in the knees at the sight of a man. Yet, Axel. *Axel.* She stopped to catch her breath. She glanced back. Was he following her? He was nowhere in sight, and she let out a breath she hadn't been aware of holding. He'd given up.

"Good," she murmured. Though a sense of disappointment lodged in her chest. Why? She bit her lip, adjusted her purse, and continued on her way. Why was she disappointed? Damn therapist making her analyze her every move.

Why was she disappointed? Because she desired him. And she'd never had a man like him show any interest in her. Really, men hardly showed interest in her at all. She'd never been the popular girl or the one who attracted the hunk. She'd had one boyfriend in college and that had not ended well. It had lasted a year, and he'd belittled her the first chance he had.

Axel was different. He spooked her in a way which was unfamiliar yet enticing. Hadn't she told her therapist she wished she were more brazen with the opposite sex? She sighed. She should have stayed. She should have taken the risk. Her therapist would be as disappointed in her as she was.

She stopped at the entrance to the subway and glanced back. She could return. She could find him there and give him her number. She shook her head. Who was she kidding? She'd blown her chance. If she went back, he'd think she was an absolute nutcase. One moment wanting one thing and the next changing her mind. Unstable. Indecisive. Insecure. Besides, she didn't have the guts.

"Bye, Axel," she murmured.

Head down, she entered the station. There was no going back. She rushed to catch the train. Entering the wagon, she found a seat and entertained herself by doom scrolling through TikTok. Somehow, the algorithm had picked up on her mood and kept showing her videos of therapists giving advice on how to act if you met someone you liked. She shut the device off and closed her eyes, attempting to stop the myriad of thoughts racing in her brain. Axel's eyes. His grin. His smooth voice which seemed to caress every inch of her skin. Squirming in her seat, she switched to her phone again. Finally, she arrived at her stop. She walked to her apartment and hurried up the three flights of stairs. She couldn't wait to change into something more comfortable and bury her nose in a book so she could get rid of all thoughts of Axel. She turned the last corner and gasped.

The sound echoed in her ears.

"Axel."

He was here. Dressed in a leather jacket and holding a motorcycle helmet in one hand, he grinned at her. His presence at her doorstop was even more commanding than before, the small hallway suffocating her. She wasn't sure if she wanted to run into his arms or back outside.

"What? How?"

"If you'd agreed to give me your number, I wouldn't have had to track you down."

"But this. It isn't … I should," she mumbled incoherently. "Call the police."

He pulled out a familiar looking book from inside

his jacket.

"You forgot this."

"My notebook."

"That's how I found where you lived."

Relief flooded her. At least there was an explanation. This time she did move forward. She reached for her book, but he lifted it out of her reach.

"Not so fast, Baby Girl."

"It's my—"

"Personal belonging. I know, and as tempting as it was, I resisted reading anything, except the address and the first page. As soon as I saw how personal it was, I stopped." Sincerity seemed to lace his words and she couldn't help but believe him.

"Thank you," she said.

"That's more like it." He smiled. His eyes twinkled. "Now, as I have saved your notebook from the hands of an ill-intentioned reader—our barman is not the most discreet person—I think it's only fair you give me a reward."

"A reward?" Her pulse leapt.

He nodded.

"What kind of reward?"

"First, you're going to invite me inside."

Her heartbeat drummed in her ears. Invite him inside? They would be alone. The fantasies she had refused to entertain on her way home returned with full-blown force. Fear clawed its hands on the edge of her consciousness.

"I don't live alone," she said.

"No one answered when I rang," he pointed out.

"Oh, they must be out." The familiar knot in her stomach reappeared. How could she avoid this? Did she want to?

"Then what are we waiting for?" He cocked an

eyebrow and moved to one side, giving her room to open the door. She glanced at him. The knot moved lower, changing its location. Her pussy throbbed. She didn't want to send him away again. This was her second chance. Rummaging through her purse, she found the keys.

He could hurt her. Anxiety reared its ugly head again. Mock her. He couldn't want someone like her, could he? She didn't know him. He could be a killer for all she knew. She wasn't the type of girl to bring a stranger home.

The pressure of his palm on the small of her back brought her back to the moment.

"I'm not going to hurt you, Alice. Open the door. You can do it."

His soothing tone boosted her confidence. He wanted her or he wouldn't be here. She pushed her insecurities aside and finally inserted the key into the lock.

Chapter Six

Axel didn't want to remove his hand. For goodness' sake, he wanted to touch her actual skin, to run his fingertips across every inch of her body. He yearned to demand she kneel before him and suck him off.

He was well aware that for the time being, it would have to remain a fantasy. He hadn't read her notebook. He'd been truthful. Reading one page had been enough. His Baby Girl had anxiety, and everything scared her. The last thing he wanted was to join that list of frightening things. No, he had to gain her trust, to show her he would be her support, not something to flee from. He had no idea how he was going to do that without fucking her brains out, but he had to try.

They entered the small apartment, and he reluctantly let go of her as she switched on the lights.

"It's small," she said apologetically. "New York is expensive and—"

"There's no need to apologize. I lived in the city too and I was young and broke once."

"Um … you were?"

He laughed.

"I haven't always been forty." He made his way to her worn gray couch. Setting some throw pillows to one side, he sat down. "Yes, I paid my way through college and then got into, er, art consulting before I made enough money to open the bar."

"How long has it been open?"

"A few years. I met, some … um," he hesitated unsure if he should tell her. "Other shifters," he finally said. Honesty was the best policy and there was no point in denying the truth from his mate. His heart skipped several beats as he waited for her to say something. He could sense her unease. Her gaze darted left and right and the vein in her neck throbbed in quick pulses.

"You must have questions," he gently prodded her.

"I don't want to be rude."

"You won't be." He smiled encouragingly.

"What are you?" Her gaze lifted to his and dropped just as quickly. Her cheeks reddened and she hurried to busy herself picking up the contents of the coffee table.

"A lion."

The glass she had been holding smashed into a thousand pieces. She cursed quietly and bent over to retrieve it. He stood and placed his palm on top of her head. She froze. Desire coursed through him. One pull and she'd be at his crotch, one kiss away. *Not yet, you pervert.* He sunk his fingers in her hair and bit back a growl of satisfaction. Tugging lightly, he forced her to lift her head. She met his gaze, her eyes wide.

"Don't be afraid, Baby Girl." Slowly, he crouched so they were eye to eye. "I'm not going to hurt you, Alice. Never." He released her hair and slid his hand down to cup her cheek. Grasping her chin, he kept her eyes pinned to his. "Tell me what is on your mind."

She tried to shake her head, but his grip was tight. "No," she said hoarsely.

"Tell me," he demanded, lowering his voice an octave. Fear danced in her gentle brown eyes. "I will not judge you." She shut her eyes, but he'd already seen tears gathering at the corners.

"You won't?" she murmured.

"Never," he said vehemently.

A long sigh escaped her body, and she softened in his grip. Somehow, she trusted him and it made his chest burst with pride.

"You're the king of the jungle, and kings—lions—always have many, um, lionesses."

"It might be so in the animal world, but we are something different. We have mates, Baby Girl, for life. No other is as alluring to us besides our mate. And then we have family." He hesitated. "Our pack. Our pride."

"There are more like you?"

"Yes. I have a pride."

"Oh."

"They are there when you need them. They have your back. We work together, but in the end, we are like any other family."

"I see."

"What about your family?"

She finally looked at him. He released her and she resumed picking up the pieces of glass.

"They're nice. I love them. They're family."

"But?" he encouraged her to continue.

She gave him a fleeting smile and his heart almost burst from within its constraints. The animal within him purred, pleased with the progress.

"They're critical. Nothing is good enough for them."

"So, you've been brought up with the idea you should be perfect."

"Yeah, I guess."

"No one is perfect."

"That's what my therapist says." She snorted.

"But you are practically perfect for me."

Her gaze reminded him of a trapped prey, wide-eyed and desperate. She scrambled to her feet.

"I'm going to throw this out," she declared.

He allowed her to go to the kitchen alone. Standing back up, he sat on the couch again and took in the petite apartment. It was cozy, with some photos of the two girls who shared it on the wall along with a large-sized print of Henry Matisse's, *Cat With Red Fish*. He wondered if she was an art enthusiast. If she was, she'd love his place.

Patience, Axel.

They had made progress but there was no way she'd agree to go there, yet.

"Would you like something to drink?" she called from the kitchen.

"A glass of water would be nice."

He heard her opening and closing cupboards, no doubt taking time to calm herself. Finally, she returned with two glasses of water in her hand.

"Here." Just as she approached him, she tripped, sending part of the water splashing over him.

"I'm so sorry," she exclaimed. She stared, obviously embarrassed and apparently unsure of what to do.

Axel chuckled. He took the glasses from her and placed them on the coffee table.

"Show me to the bathroom."

She nodded and hurried down the hall. He followed.

"Here. I'll get a clean towel." He entered the blue-tiled bathroom. His shirt was wet, but it was by no means drenched. Nonetheless, a devious plan began to form in his mind. His beast mewled in satisfaction. He undid the buttons on his shirt and took it off. He didn't need to turn around to know she had returned. Her gasp filled the space.

"Here," she murmured. She stuck out the towel at arm's length. He took a step forward coming into contact with the material.

"You got me wet. You should dry me."

"What?" She stared at him but didn't run away.

Progress.

He grasped her wrist, gliding her hand across his chest. Her fingers flexed. Her lips parted. He slid the towel across his body. Her gaze became hooded. Her heart pounded. Intense. Wild. It called to him. His cock hardened. Her scent wafted up his nose. Desire spiraled through him. The beast within him purred. *More. More.*

"That's it," he cooed.

Taking her other hand, he pressed her open palm to his pec. She didn't resist. A low whisper of a moan escaped her lips. He growled in response. She glanced at him.

"This—"

"Is very good," he praised her. "Continue, Baby Girl."

Her gaze dropped again, and she focused on his chest. Slowly he released his grip on her. To his delight, she continued to caress him, almost like in a trance. He touched her shoulder, and she froze.

"Don't stop, Baby Girl."

"You have so many tattoos." Her hand fell to her side.

He swore at himself for his impatience. He should have continued to let her explore at her own pace.

"Yes. They paint a picture of who I am. This one"—he pointed to the half-geometric lion below his heart—"is the symbol of my pride."

"And that one?"

She pointed to the triskelion.

He frowned. He could lie, but what was the point?

"My tendencies in bed. BDSM."

Her cheeks reddened so fast he thought she was going to faint.

"Oh, wow. I didn't mean to pry."

He grabbed her before she could run away and

pulled her right against him. Her gasp was music to his ears, but the fact she didn't try to get away from him was solace to his soul. He gently grasped her chin, forcing her gaze to him. Her pupils were dilated and her lips parted. Axel pushed the urge to kiss her to one side. Not yet.

"Have you ever tried BDSM?"

"No."

"Would you like to?"

She averted her gaze. "No."

"You're lying, Alice. Don't lie to me, Baby Girl." He lowered his tone to a deep whisper. "I will always know."

Chapter Seven

Alice's heart was going to come out of her chest. She was pressed against him so she could feel every curve and hardness in his body. Her pussy was soaked, pulsing with the need to be filled. But it was his gaze and the tone of his voice that kept her captive. She couldn't look away. She couldn't lie to him. She believed him when he said he'd always known.

"I have fantasized about it," she admitted.

"Good girl," he rumbled. Her chest tightened at the words. "How did that make you feel?" he asked.

She swallowed hard. "Good," she admitted.

"Do you want more?"

Heat traveled from her head to her toes.

"Yes," she said.

His gaze lit up like a rekindled flame.

"I'm going to kiss you," he said, softly. "You're going to accept it."

She nodded.

"I want you to say it. Yes." He seemed to hesitate. "Yes, Daddy."

Fire coursed through her. She could no longer tell if it was mortification or desire. She wet her lips. His gaze darkened. Pleasure coursed through her.

"Yes, Daddy."

The words came out with surprising ease. A smile flitted over Axel's lips, and a sense of calm washed over her. He would take care of her. He would protect her. *Axel.*

He brushed his lips against hers. A moan lodged at the back of her throat from the mere contact.

"Alice, Baby Girl," he murmured.

He pressed them to her mouth again, this time

more forcefully. She whimpered.

"*Alice, are you home? Alice! OMG, you're not going to believe this.*"

Her world shattered at the sound of the familiar voice. The door slammed shut and the clapping of heels on the floor filled her senses. A sliver of fear and shame ran through her. She veered around but wasn't fast enough. Her roommate had already seen them. Axel, shirtless in her bathroom. She was in his arms, all but ready to kiss him, no doubt bright red.

"Alice, what is going on?" Nessa practically shrieked.

Her friend stared at them from the doorway, her jaw almost on the floor.

"Nessa," she shrieked out the name. "You're…"

Nessa grinned.

"I'm so sorry," she fussed. "I didn't realize you had a visitor. I'll go." She backed out of the hallway chuckling.

"No!" Alice cried, struggling out of Axel's grip. He released her immediately. Reality came crashing down around her. The knot in her stomach returned with fury. She was in her apartment with a virtual stranger, and they had been about to kiss. Her skin burned and a tremble coursed through her body. Her roommate had caught them in the act. What would she think? She wanted the floor to swallow her whole. Instead, words spewed out of her mouth without control.

"Nessa. Axel was just about to leave. He came to return my notebook. I left it at the bar and then he asked for some water, and I spilled it on him, and I was bringing him a towel. We hardly know each other. Nothing is happening. He … it wasn't—"

She stiffened at the warm touch of his fingertips on her shoulders, but the flow of words died. She stared at Nessa, who stood next to the couch with a big grin on her face.

"It's okay, Alice," she said. "I'll leave."

"No." Axel interjected. "I'll go." He squeezed her shoulder. "Breathe," he whispered. As if on command she let out a long breath. "Alice, you will see me to the door."

"Yes, of course," she replied. A moment later, she realized it hadn't been a question.

He walked past without another word. Alice stared after him. Longing assaulted her system, taking her by surprise. She didn't want him to leave. Did she? Nessa nudged her on the ribs.

"Are you sure you don't want me to leave?" she whispered. She winked at her. "You never bring anyone over, and you looked busy."

"Yes, it's fine. Shut up," she replied coarsely.

Axel stood at the door waiting for her. Turning to Nessa, he extended his hand. "It has been a pleasure to meet you, Nessa, albeit in strange circumstances."

Her friend flushed and a flash of jealousy ran through her. Alice frowned. She crossed her arms over her chest. Had he done something to her?

"Alice."

He extended his palm to her. Hesitantly, she took it. Bending over it, he kissed the top of her hand. His lips were soft and gentle. There was no pressure, no demand. He glanced up at her, his fiery eyes piercing.

"We shall stay in touch." He didn't say it aloud, but he didn't need to. The words "Baby Girl" lingered in the air. Heat infused every cell in her body and the urge to tell him to stay crossed her mind. She pushed it away and pulled back her hand, aware that Nessa was still standing a few feet behind her.

"Bye."

Giving them both a brief nod, he picked up his

helmet and walked out. As soon as the door shut, Nessa turned to her.

"Alice, what the fuck?"

"I don't know. I'm sorry," she began to apologize though she wasn't even sure what she was doing it for.

"Girl, I know you haven't had anyone over, but him? He could be your father. Did you see the gray in his hair? I mean, he's a hunky silver fox, to be fair, but how old is he? Fifty?"

"Forty."

"Forty!" Nessa kicked off her shoes. "He was no doubt looking to take advantage of you. A sweet, innocent, twenty-something. Those men are predators. You should be more careful."

"Yes," she said.

Nessa continued ranting without paying attention to her. "Did you go to that bar Hannah told you about? Was that where you met him? I knew that bar was fishy. A gin bar? I mean, come on, that's for old people."

"I..." Alice was at a loss for words. The gray in his hair. Yes, he had a few silver strands in the reddish mane he sported, but Nessa was taking it too far. Wasn't she? "He—"

"I know you haven't been on a date in ages with your anxiety and everything, but I'm sure you can do better than that." Her friend walked to the living room and threw herself on the couch. "I'm going to take you out to a real party to meet some men our age. You really need to go out more anyway. Didn't your therapist say so? I'm sure she would disapprove of the gray-haired grandpa."

She nodded automatically, but Alice wanted to scream. *"Nessa!"* she wanted to cry out. *"It's none of your business who I date. You're always dating deadbeat losers and getting your heart broken."* Instead, she remained quiet. Her heart racing and her palm and lips tingling where Axel had touched them. She glanced at the door. She wanted him to return and finish what they had started. This had been her second chance, and she had blown it again, allowing shame to control her life. The crushing weight of reality settled on her shoulders. She'd blown it. Once again, instead of taking the plunge she'd panicked and sent what she wanted away, missing out on something which could have been amazing.

"And even if it wasn't, at least you would have tried." Her therapist's voice seemed to whisper in her ear once more.

Well, it was too late now. He was gone. The moment had passed and would never repeat itself. She fought back the tears and struggled to pay attention to Nessa who was going on and on about her date that night with a financial analyst who was apparently loaded.

Focus, Alice.

His parting words snaked their way into her mind. *"We'll be in touch."* Her heart skipped a beat. Would he fulfill his promise? Would she have another chance?

VOLUME FOUR

Chapter Eight

Axel rode his motorcycle through the city. The warm wind swept at him, and he bit back a frustrated growl. He needed to get away from the asphalt jungle and go for a run, let out some of the pent-up anger and frustration his lion was holding in. It had taken all his control not to grab Alice and kiss her senselessly in that bathroom. He'd managed to hold back and then her friend had come barging in.

Friend? He snorted. The young woman was very clearly a narcissist, only interested in hearing the sound of her own voice. If she had been a true friend, she would have kept her opinion to herself or at least until Alice had asked her for it. Unfortunately, his Baby Girl was too afraid of others to stand up for herself. Her fear kept her from enjoying life to the fullest. He didn't know where it stemmed from, but he would do anything to take it away from her and make her live. He skipped his usual exit to his city apartment since it was being renovated and instead continued onto the highway, heading to his pride lands. There, he would run and relax for a bit and come up with a new plan to conquer his mate.

One hour later, he parked in his driveway. He didn't bother going into the house. He rid himself of his clothes. Sweat coated his body. He was so ready for this. The transformation was painless, the limbs readjusting, fur growing at the speed of light. He'd barely completed the shift, he set off at a run, enjoying the feel of the earth on his paws. This wasn't the savannah, but he'd take it over anything else. Here, they had the privacy they needed to be who they really were. Here, at home, they could shift and run free. This was the central home to his pride. All of them could come here whenever they wanted and enjoy this freedom. The smell of the dirt and the trees around him filled his nostrils. He didn't need anything else, except his mate. He roared in agony at the thought of her. She wanted him but she was so far from him. He picked up the speed, fighting the thoughts. He spotted a rabbit and ran after it to get his mind off things. Finally, tired out, he climbed a tree.

The image of Alice came to him, and he mewled with desperation. How the hell was he going to get Alice, such a frail creature, to accept being part of a lion pack? Though she wouldn't have the ability to shift, she would become the leader of the pride at his side. Would the other lions accept her? Most importantly, would she accept herself? He could protect her from the others, but not from herself. That was something she would have to do on her own.

He sighed.

The mating ritual was easy. He had to mark her as his, but she had to claim him as well. With her fearful nature, he could already picture her refusing him, stating for a reason that she wasn't good enough, and condemning them both to a loveless life.

Alice. What had hurt her? He wanted to protect her from all pain, from all loss and fear, and make sure she never suffered again. Yet, he couldn't. Why was life so damn complicated sometimes? Just a few days ago he had been out in the city fucking whomever he wanted however he wanted, mindless of love or mating, and now he was here, desiring the only woman who seemed to be afraid of her own shadow.

He let out a frustrated roar. Scared, a flock of birds took to the sky. He followed their trajectory to another tree.

He was exasperated, but he would not back down. He hadn't gotten to where he was in life by giving up.

He climbed down from the tree and began walking back to his clothes. He glanced at the mansion in the distance. He hadn't even considered the other factors in his life. He would have to explain his business to her —how he had made his fortune. He shook his head. None of that mattered. The first thing he had to do was conquer the damsel. Once that was done, everything else would follow.

He would get Alice to be his Baby Girl and his queen.

VOLUME FOUR

Chapter Nine

Alice lay awake in bed. She stared at the ceiling. She didn't know how long she'd been tossing and turning. She couldn't calm her thoughts or her body.

She had gone to bed shortly after Nessa had arrived, complaining of a headache. Really, she just wanted to be alone with her thoughts. She was restless. She had tried journaling, but the words were not flowing so she'd opted to play some soothing music and try to get some sleep. It wasn't working. Her thoughts raced in all directions.

First, she replayed the encounter with Axel in the bar. What if she had said yes to him then? Would they have ended in a back room? His hot mouth on hers. His firm torso pressed to her breasts. The space too small for them to maneuver but enough for them to satiate the heat coursing through them.

She groaned and turned to one side. He was a shifter. She wasn't sure what that meant. The new species had come out recently and not a lot was known about them, except that they could change at will into other creatures. Some of them hunted.

Did Axel hunt? Where? And weren't lions notorious for having a pride? He'd said he had one. The tattoo on his chest was the symbol of his pack. Weren't male lions accompanied exclusively by female lions? Was that why he had been accompanied by those women at the bar? Were they part of his pride? Were the scantily dressed women lionesses at his beck and call? Where did that leave her?

It couldn't be. Could it? He was too old for them. Old. Nessa had said so and she was right. *Old enough to be your father.* She didn't know if that was the case, but she felt as if it didn't matter. So, what if he was older? He had more experience, more knowledge. At his side she could navigate this world fearlessly. It didn't matter that he was older. He was more mature. More worldly. She was the problem. She was too young. She didn't have a lot to offer. She was a recent graduate, working to survive and little more. She liked to read, doom scroll through her phone, and occasionally hang out with her friends. What could she offer him that he didn't have or that he could find elsewhere? He'd lived countless adventures, she was certain. She was boring in comparison. Nothing. She had nothing to offer.

She turned to the other side, brushing her breast in the process.

Except one thing. He seemed to be interested in that: her sex. She lay on her back. Why was she worrying about offering him anything else? He hadn't asked. This wasn't about love. It wasn't about partnership. Heck, it wasn't even about friendship. She didn't know him, and he didn't know her. There was only one thing that tied them together. Sex.

He had demonstrated an unabashed sexual interest in her. She could have a one-night fling. Right? She'd never had one before, but surely she could manage. It would have been perfect if Nessa hadn't arrived when she did. With the momentum ruined she'd recovered her bearings and that brief moment where she'd felt endless peace in his arms, vanished. She couldn't go on. All that was left of her encounter was a pair of wet panties and a sense of shame. But he was gone now and so was Nessa. She was alone in her room. She could dream. Pretend they would find each other again and when they did, he'd kiss her senseless. Her breath would be stolen from her lungs and her knees would buckle but he'd catch her. "Baby Girl," he'd whisper.

"Daddy," Alice murmured in the darkness of her bedroom.

He caressed her cheeks, his fingertips soft and arousing every inch of her body from the simple touch. She arched into him, silently beckoning for more.

"That's my good girl." He stopped at her neck. She glanced at him. Slowly, he reached lower, opening the first button of her shirt. She bit her bottom lip to keep from moaning.

He dipped lower. One by one, he popped the buttons, until there were none left. He opened her shirt, exposing her breasts.

"Beautiful," he muttered. "Take off the shirt, Baby Girl."

She would comply without a word, casting it aside. In her bedroom, she rid herself of her pajama t-shirt.

"Unzip your skirt. Slowly."

"Yes, Daddy."

She reached behind her and unzipped the gray pencil skirt. Shimming, she allowed it to drop to her ankles.

"Come here."

Suddenly, she switched the location of her fantasy. They were no longer in her home. They were back at the bar. He was sitting down on one of the low velvet chairs. The soft jazzy music filled the ambiance, but they were the only ones there.

"Come, Baby Girl." He patted his lap.

She made his way to him, naked except for her panties and bra.

"Dance for me, Alice." He smirked, and she smiled in response. The confidence she never had in real life washing over her in this fantasy.

Allowing herself to be washed over by the music,

she began to move her hips. She moved closer to him, gyrating. She stood with her back to him swiveling her ass from side to side over the erection clearly outlined on his pants. His large hands grabbed her hips, taking control of her movements. He lowered her further, rubbing her pussy against his hard dick. She moaned.

"Turn around, Baby Girl."

"Yes, Daddy."

She did as he asked, and he brought her down to sit on him. Another moan burst through her lips at the contact. His lips found hers, kissing her hard. She whimpered against him. He undid her bra, her nipples hardening even further in the cool air.

In her bedroom, Alice squeezed the taught tips and groaned.

"Daddy," she murmured. "Axel."

She pictured his mouth on her breast, sucking one turgid point and then another. Her hips rolled over her bed, and she slid her other hand to her moist pussy. She began to rub her clit.

"Daddy, please."

"Tell me what you want."

"Fuck me, please," she begged shamelessly.

"No. Get off on me, Baby Girl." He began to rock her against the outline of his cock. "I want to see you come by your own hand, Baby Girl."

She nodded. Her eyes drifted shut. She rubbed her pussy, sliding her fingers beneath her panties. Faster and harder, picturing the outline of his cock rubbing against her clit. She bit back the moan lodged in her throat, aware that Nessa was in the other room.

"Daddy, please."

"Come, Baby Girl, let me hear you scream."

Her hips lifted and fell, her orgasm washing over her in a wave. She bit her other hand, moaning out his name, "Axel."

Moments later, Alice opened her eyes and removed her hand from between her legs. Her pussy still pulsated from the orgasm. She groaned and punched the pillow. Surely, she would never see him again, but at least she had her fantasies.

VOLUME FOUR

Chapter Ten

Alice snoozed her alarm clock and turned to one side. She couldn't remember if she'd dreamt anything but whatever it was, she was sure it had involved Axel. Her alarm clock rang again, and she turned it off. Her eyes widened as she realized the time. Shit. She was going to be late. She rushed to get dressed and practically ran out the door.

Luckily, she barely arrived five minutes late to work but when she walked through the door the commotion startled her.

"What's happened?" she asked the receptionist.

"OMG, Alice. You happened." She pointed excitedly at the enormous bouquet of flowers covering her desk.

"What?" she murmured. Her face flushed. Heat ran through her body. Confusion mingled with embarrassment.

"Alice," another colleague yelled out her name. "Dish out! Who's the admirer?"

She ignored her and unsteadily made her way to the desk. The folded envelope with her name on it caught her eye.

"Aren't you going to open it?"

"Yes," she managed to croak out. I'm admiring the flowers."

"Open it, open it," someone chanted.

"Maybe we should let her open it privately and go back to work." Her boss popped out of nowhere giving everyone a stern look. The gossipers mumbled an apology and walked out. Her boss then looked at her. "I know you have no fault in it, but tell your admirer not to do it again. It disrupts the office."

"Of course. I'm sorry," she murmured.

Apparently satisfied, her boss returned to his desk. Finally alone, she sat down. Trembling slightly, she picked up the envelope.

Good job, Baby Girl. I imagine the ruckus this bouquet might have created, and I apologize. See you tonight at 7PM at the bar.

Yours Always, Axel – Daddy.

Her heart skipped several beats. *Daddy.* Last night's fantasy burned brightly in her mind. She pressed her legs together, her pussy tingling in remembrance.

Tonight? Was that an invitation? It wasn't phrased like a question. So, it was an order? She couldn't quite decide. Both? He'd included his phone number at the bottom. Should she write to him? Shoot. She should refuse. He was ordering her about and they hardly knew each other. Surely, that was a red flag. Nessa wouldn't like it. *"Too old and bossy,"* she'd say. The issue was, she enjoyed being told what to do, and she didn't think he was that old.

She put the card in her purse. She had the option not to go. She didn't have to obey. Yet, she wanted to. Every fiber in her being was compelled to do as he asked. Surely, this was her last chance. How many more opportunities could the universe grant her?

She stared at her laptop. She had to work, though how she would manage to do so all day was beyond her.

****

Somehow, she made it. She'd sat through the day and ignored the curious glances from her colleague, or the occasional pestering question. She didn't know if it had anything to do with the letter because every time she glanced at it, or felt nerves assaulting her, she'd remember the first words: *Good girl, Baby Girl.* How could a set of four words calm her? By the end of the day, she'd decided it wasn't the words, it was the man behind them. Knowing that Axel was the one saying them was what kept her grounded. He was counting on her to be a good girl. She couldn't disappoint him.

Alice stepped onto the street. The Gin Room was a few blocks away. Yesterday, she'd walked there. Anxiety kicked her in the stomach like a freight train. It was time. He was waiting for her. She had saved his phone number, but she hadn't responded to the card because she wasn't sure if she'd go or not. What if he had left? What if he'd decided she wasn't coming? She should have responded. She bit her lip. It hadn't been a question. He was waiting and this was her final chance. What did they say? Third time's the charm?

That was it.

VOLUME FOUR

Chapter Eleven

Axel took in the blueprints laid out in front of him. He couldn't focus properly, and he knew why. *Alice.*

She'd haunted his dreams and all his waking moments. He'd sent the flowers on a whim, only realizing his terrible mistake when he was filling out the card details. She would hate him for making her the center of attention. Would she forgive him? He'd hoped that by leaving his phone number she'd get in touch with him, but he'd heard nothing from her all day.

Surely, she felt the connection too. The desire which burned deep within them, and which would only be sated once they mated. God, he hoped it was soon. He needed her. The urge to regain his wits was pressing. He had work to do, and not only the bar.

He hadn't lied to her when he'd told her he'd worked his way through college. He had. He simply hadn't mentioned what he had been doing.

Art thievery.

Back then, shifting was still hidden to the general public. He was an unknown and he had taken advantage of his prowess to get into places and steal what was asked of him: rare and valuable pieces of art. He'd made a lot of money and eventually started to meet others who were also into the same thing. His pride had formed. He'd become the king of the pride, and before he knew it, they had become a well-known art gang. He rarely did any thieving nowadays, that's what he had a pride for, but occasionally he took the odd job here and there, and he supervised all his family's work to ensure success.

He glanced at the blueprints again. It was Alice's office building. That's how he'd known where she worked. He'd caught a glimpse of her work badge the other night. His client wanted a piece of art the CEO of the company had in his office. Apparently, it hadn't been painted by a famous artist, but it was unique. According to his client, the missing piece to his collection.

Axel's client had told him he'd tried to buy it from the CEO but hadn't been able to. So, he'd come to him.

Access to the building wasn't hard, but the mission had two major problems. One was getting to the top floor and then out. The second was the hyenas. Natural lion enemies, they worked at the building and were quick-witted. It wasn't the first time the predator shifters got in their way—nor would it be the last.

He checked the time again. Alice should be about to arrive. He rehearsed his plan. Talk to her and invite her out to dinner. That was it. He had to take things slowly with Alice or she'd panic. A night out where they could relax and get to know each other more intimately was perfect. The lion within him roared with displeasure, sending a jolt of pain across his spine.

The beast wanted more, but it was going to have to wait.

Abruptly, the sting dissipated. Axel sniffed the air. She had arrived. Her unique scent tinged with fear reached him. The animal was already attuned to her presence even if his human side still had a fight ahead of him

Axel folded the blueprints and stuck them into the pocket of his jacket. He had to make a move soon, but right now, Alice was his priority.

Chapter Twelve

What was she doing here? Alice hesitated at the door. Nerves made her fingertips tingle unpleasantly. Her heart thrummed in her ears erratically.

The bar hadn't changed, except for one thing: it was packed. Right and left people sat around or stood, chatting amicably, almost drowning out the suave music. The knot in her stomach began to tighten. Someone could approach her, speak to her, and then what? Maybe this hadn't been such a good idea. She took a step back. Suddenly, she felt it.

His gaze was like fire calling to a moth. She turned toward the pull. How he had known she'd arrived was beyond her, but there he was, waiting. He stood at the doorway to the VIP area. Their gazes locked. Her fantasies didn't do him justice. Today he wore a white shirt open at the top, giving an enticing glimpse of his chest, along with dark jeans. His hair was pulled back into a man-bun, adding to his attraction.

She swallowed hard. He beckoned her with a finger, and she moved forward, her feet almost moving on their own accord. She stopped a hair's breadth away from him. His grin undid her, and her breath jammed in the back of her throat.

"Good girl."

She almost moaned at the words. So simple and yet so powerful. No one had ever called her a good girl. All her life, all she got was constant criticism. As a child she was told she was not good enough. Bullied by her peers, she was too fat, too tall, too weird. Her parents always thought she didn't study enough. *"You should be getting A+, not A- or B+. It's not good enough."* As an adult at university, she had had teachers telling her she could do better. Her classmates criticized her work. It wasn't good enough. Nothing ever was. No one had told her she had done well. That it was enough. No one had praised her and called her a good girl. *Except him.* This man, this stranger, for that was what he still was, had reached within her and drawn out an aching need she had ignored for years with two simple words.

"Come in, Baby Girl."

Alice followed him inside without a word. She didn't know what to say or how to act. Doubts still assaulted her. What was he expecting of her? Would they just kiss? Have sex? Maybe he didn't want any of that. Maybe this was some kind of game for him. After all, he was a wealthy man, older than her by at least fifteen years, and she was nothing more than a puppet in his hands, a mere toy to play with and later discard. Could she even do this?

"Sit." He pointed at the dark leather sofa in the room and headed to a minibar in the corner. She obeyed. She sat stiffly, watching him as he poured two glasses of brown liquid. He handed one to her. "Drink."

Abruptly, her sense of preservation snapped into her. "What is it?" She cleared her throat. "What is it?" she repeated.

"Cognac. Drink a sip." He took one himself. "It'll help you relax."

"Why do I need to relax?"

He gave her a lopsided smile.

"Because you're so nervous if I were to touch you right now, you'd snap like a wooden board. Drink," he said again. A shiver ran through her. Had he lowered his voice or was it her imagination? She swallowed drily and glanced at the glass in her hand. What if it were drugged? She had been watching him prepare it but—

"I didn't put anything in it. I don't need to, Alice.

Coming here has been your own decision, and what's more, in case you have any doubts, I would never dare hurt you." He paused. "Not in that way." The sly grin that crossed his features made her cheeks warm and this time she did take a sip. She coughed, surprised at the strong flavor. He chuckled. "I take it you hadn't drunk this before."

"No," she said. Tears gathered at the corner of her eyes. He handed her a handkerchief and took the glass from her, replacing it with another in seconds. "Drink. It's water."

Trusting him, and uncomfortable with the burning in her throat, she gulped down the contents. The cool liquid soothed her immediately. "Thanks."

"I will never hurt you, Alice." He stared at her, and she shivered involuntarily. She dropped her gaze, nervously toying with the empty glass in her hand. Her mind reeled with a jumble of thoughts she couldn't organize. She surprised herself when words formed on her tongue and tumbled out.

"But you want to." It wasn't a question, it was a statement.

Axel nodded. "Very much so. I want to tug on your hair and spread your mouth around my cock. I want to tie your hands over your head and spank you until your entire backside is red as a rose." He took in an audibly shaky breath. "I want to hurt you, but I also want to love you." Without giving her a chance, he continued, "I want to caress every inch of your body, hold you in my arms, and keep you safe from all harm, both outside and inside." Axel tapped his head. "I want to make you forget your pain, your fears, and just enjoy, live the moment with me."

Alice stared at him wide-eyed. He spoke of more than sex. She tried to make sense of everything he'd said, but only the last words seemed to stick with her.

"I want to make you forget your pain, your fears, and just enjoy, live the moment with me."

"I don't know if I can do that," she whispered. "Living in the moment," she hurried to explain. Dread clawed at her neck, scratching its way downward. She attempted to push it aside, focusing on the rest of his confession. Sex. Being tied, spanked, but also caressed. Her pussy tingled. "Well, and the rest ... I've never—"

"I will teach you," he assured her. Axel crouched so he was staring at her eye to eye. "I will keep you safe, Baby Girl." He cupped her cheek, and she bit back a gasp. Soft, velvety spirals of electricity seemed to shoot from his fingertips onto her flesh. Warm and delicate, they invited her to sink further.

"Every time you touch me..." she murmured. She placed her hand over his. "I just ... I don't understand."

Axel nodded.

"I know, and there's a lot for me to explain, but this is not the place. Would you be willing to come to my home?"

Alice stared at him. Her mind was turmoil, but even though apprehension still twisted her gut, the warmth in his gaze was a welcome pool she dove into instinctively.

"Yes," she heard herself answer.

Chapter Thirteen

Normally, people would describe him as calm, laid-back, but fierce when needed. Axel believed this was the first time he'd jumped the gun. He'd laid everything on her. What he wanted to do to her physically and emotionally. To boot, he'd invited her to his home to do it. He was certain she wouldn't accept. After all, he hadn't taken the time to build her trust, which from the little he knew of his Alice, was something she required. However, the moment he'd had her close, the second he'd touched her, the animal within him had taken control. More and more the lion wanted her, needed her to be his. Every minute stretched like an hour without completing the mating.

Alice had to feel it too or she wouldn't have come or even touched him. He had the impression everything she'd done to this point was going against her character. It was insanity, and yet neither of them could stop it.

"Yes," she said.

The widening of her gaze betrayed her surprise. His beast let out a satisfied roar within its confines, sending a flash of pleasure darting through his system. Axel clasped Alice's hand and kissed the top. She shivered and he smiled, pleased at her reaction. The fact they were running a wild race didn't matter—doing it together was the key.

"Have you ever ridden a motorcycle?" he asked.

Alice's jaw dropped.

"No."

"Guess today will be a day of many firsts. Come on." He pulled her to her feet. She rose unsteadily, balancing herself with a hand on his chest. His lion mewled with delight at the touch, and he tugged her closer. She froze.

"I'm sorry. I didn't mean to—" she blurted.

"There's no need to apologize, Baby Girl. You can touch me all you want." He slid her hand to his open collar. She didn't fight him, her digits flexing on his flesh. Her lips parted inviting a kiss. His lion roared, demanding more.

"I…" she whispered. "This." She shook her head slightly. "I can't breathe."

Axel clenched his jaw. Her breathless words slammed him back to the reality of the moment. What was he doing? He had to take things slowly. He took an unwilling step back.

"It's okay, Baby Girl. One breath at a time. In through your nose, count to four, now out."

Alice followed his rhythm. "That's right." He held her hand and squeezed. "Easy does it."

After a few seconds, she finally managed to give him a weak smile.

"Thanks." Her cheeks burned. "It wasn't really a panic attack. I just, well, touching you…" She left the sentence hanging.

Axel chuckled.

"Trust me, I feel the same way. Are you ready, then?"

She nodded. Relief swept through him, and he let out a breath of relief he'd been unaware of holding. Not only did she also want him, she still desired to leave with him.

"Let's go." Grabbing his helmet and leather jacket, he led her through the back door of the bar to an alley where he kept his bike.

"This is it."

Alice remained rooted on the spot, staring at the vehicle as if it were an alien contraption.

"It doesn't bite, I promise." Opening the helmet lock, he pulled out his spare helmet. "Here, you must wear this."

She took it but still didn't move.

"Let me help you."

Gently, he brushed back her hair and adjusted the hat onto her head. He swallowed, fighting the urge to steal a kiss. Instead, he turned and put on his own protection. Getting onto the motorcycle, he reached for her hand.

"One foot up and then the other," he instructed, steadying her. "That's it. Hold on to me. Tightly."

He revved up the engine.

"The most important thing you must remember is that when we hit a curve, you lean toward it, okay?"

"Yes," she replied, pressing herself closer to him. A sigh escaped him. She was here. This would work out. *Eventually.*

He hit the road, enjoying the wind on his face and the warmth of her body behind him. This would be their future. He grinned, happiness covering him like a warm blanket. He took a bend, and she did as he instructed, albeit he didn't miss her yelp of fear.

Slowly, Axel.

He hadn't caught his prey yet. Finally, after what seemed to him an endless ride, they reached his home. He hit the remote and the heavy gates opened slowly. Her gasp was audible in his ears.

"You live here?"

He rode through the dimly lit driveway trying to take in the sites like a newcomer would. A golden sea of tall grass sprawled in both directions dotted with trees and shrubs. The starry sky was clear above them, almost devoid of any light pollution. Finally, as they approached the end of the road, the large Southern style house came into view.

"Welcome to my pride lands, Baby Girl."

Chapter Fourteen

Alice couldn't believe it. Axel lived in a mansion. She walked next to him, dazzled by the sheer size of the house in front of them. He unlocked the door and invited her inside. Her jaw dropped when the lights came on. The chandelier glowed softly over marble floors and a sweeping grand staircase which curved upward. In the center, an ornate pedestal had an arrangement of bright yellow and orange flowers. She turned an almost full circle, taking in the set of archways which led to other rooms.

"You live here? But you only own a bar. How?"

"Hasn't he told you it's a bit more than that?"

She spun around at the sound of the female voice. Atop the staircase stood a smiling woman with luxurious golden locks. She was dressed in tight black leggings and a turtleneck which hugged her curves and accented her beauty somehow. The low growl coming from Axel had the hair on the back of her neck stand. He touched her lower back possessively.

"Scarlet, what are you doing here?"

The woman began walking down the stairs.

"This is the pride home, Sir." She gave him a smile and a brief nod. "There's also been a problem. We needed to speak to you but couldn't reach you on your phone or in your city home since it's being renovated, so the next logical step was to come here."

Axel reached inside his coat.

"Shit," he mumbled. "I must have left my phone in the bar."

Scarlet chuckled.

"Clearly, you've had your mind elsewhere." She gave Alice a once-over. Alice felt her cheeks redden.

"What has happened?" Axel asked.

Scarlet raised an eyebrow.

"Perhaps we should speak in private," she said.

Axel frowned and sighed deeply. "I'm sorry Alice, I need to tend to this." He took her hand and squeezed it. "I wasn't expecting this, or I wouldn't have brought you here," he said.

Alice nodded dumbly.

"Of course," she agreed automatically. "I'll call an Uber and be out of your way."

"No." He grasped her shoulders tightly and looked into her eyes. "I don't want you to leave. I just need you to wait, Baby Girl."

"But you ... she ... me," she babbled incoherently. Her mind raced. He wanted her to stay?

"There are no buts. There is no she. It's just you and me. Understand?" He waited for her to nod. "Now, you're going to be a good girl and wait for me here. I won't be long."

"Okay," she whispered.

"Maybe she'd be better off waiting in the living room?" Scarlet pointed out. Amusement was clear in her features.

Axel scowled, giving the woman what looked like a warning gaze.

"Yes, you're right. Come, Alice." He took her hand and led her matter-of-factly under one of the arches. Alice couldn't hide her gasp. The room they entered was a blend of luxury and comfort. The marble floors were softened with a plush rug. The oversized leather sofas full of throw pillows invited comfort. A grand fireplace commanded attention, crowned with a striking art piece of a pride of lions.

"Wait here," Axel said. "I won't be long."

Alice nodded, too dumbfounded to say anything.

She watched them walk out together and sunk into the couch. She stared at her hands. What was happening? What did that woman want with Axel? Maybe they were romantically involved? Perhaps he had an open relationship, and he'd failed to speak to her about Alice. Jealousy snaked its way into her gut.

"What the hell?" she mumbled.

She didn't have a right to be envious of another woman. Axel was just some guy she was going to fuck. She placed her palms on her warm cheeks. Was she even sure about it? Really, she didn't know him and getting into bed with random strangers had never been her thing. Yet, she'd agreed to come here, hadn't she? She had accepted the invitation. What is more, the previous two times she'd had the chance, she'd regretted not taking it, so there was no going back. She really did want this.

She smiled. Her therapist would be proud. For once, she was certain of what she wanted, and she had taken the step to grasp it.

Alice wanted Axel. She couldn't say why. She didn't know if it was because of pheromones, hormones, or simply the fact that she felt safe with him. When she was with him, she forgot to be afraid, indecisive, anxious—or at least, as much as usual. She had been fearful when she'd gotten on the motorcycle, but as they'd ridden on, and after the first bend, she'd held onto his solid frame, casting her anxiety aside and enjoying the ride. He would take care of her. It was almost as if she could be who she really was with him and he wouldn't judge her, wouldn't run like others had.

"Who are you?"

Her head snapped up at the soft female voice. She stared at the most beautiful woman she had ever seen. She had thought the other one was incredible but surely this one was a model. At least five foot seven, she stood at the entrance to the living room dressed in curve-hugging skinny jeans and a tank top. Golden hair cascaded around her framing the face of an angel with cornflower-blue eyes and full, rosy lips. A natural luminous glow seemed to emanate from her.

"Who are you?" she repeated.

Alice realized she had been staring and blushed.

"I'm Axel's guest. He told me to wait here."

"Oh, he's home then?" She smiled, the gesture full of venom making Alice recoil. The malice in her expression darkened her features, making them almost cruel and predatory.

"I'm Ariadna, his mate," the woman said.

"Mate?" Alice echoed.

She walked into the room, nodding. Standing in front of the fireplace, she pointed at the painting and at the lioness sitting to the left of the largest lion in the picture.

"Yes. Do you know what that is?"

"I can guess," Alice murmured.

"Life mates are destined to be together. Our animals … you're not a shifter, are you?" She paused to give her a once-over. "No, you're not. Well, shifters mate. They are bound to one lover for life, and they can immediately recognize the person that completes them, the person who will lighten up their world."

Ariadna's words slapped her in the face. Fear coiled in her chest, entwining with shame. She shouldn't be here. This had all been a mistake.

"Oh, I didn't realize. I'll leave now."

"Yeah, so I'm not sure what you're doing here," Ariadna continued as if she hadn't heard her. She stood in front of her. "Unless you're a gift."

"A gift?"

Her malicious smile turned dark. She tapped her

nose as if she were nothing more than a bothersome child. "Yes, a gift to me."

Alice gaped. "I don't understand."

The woman laughed, the sound grating Alice's already frazzled nerves. She took an involuntary step back.

"We're lions, darling. We like to hunt," Ariadna said.

"Hunt?" Alice gasped. Panic squeezed her innards, nausea climbing to the back of her throat. She was rooted in place.

"Oh, yes, you must definitely be a gift." Ariadna inched closer sniffing at her neck. "I can smell the fear on you. When we let you loose on the planes you're going to run for your life, fight for survival. You'll be a thrill," the woman whispered, her warm breath caressing her ear unpleasantly and making the hairs on her arm stand.

"No, I'm no one's meal," Alice cried. She took another step. Her fight-or-flight response began to kick in. She needed to get out of there.

"Are you not? Didn't you come with Axel?"

"To fuck!" she yelled.

The woman burst out laughing.

"Darling, he could be your father. Do you really think he would go after someone like you?" She touched her lip with a perfectly manicured finger and took her in. "No, you'll be a delectable meal. As a matter a fact, I don't see why we can't start the game right now."

"Game?"

Alice screamed as the woman's features began to shift and change. Panic surged within her, and she backed up frantically. Her feet tangling on the rug, she tripped and crashed onto the floor with a cry.

This was the end.

Except, it wasn't. A massive lion jumped over her

and slammed into the lioness. They tumbled onto the floor a few feet away from her, snarling and clawing at each other. Within seconds, the lion pinned the female lion down and roared, the victorious sound echoing in the room. Then, its gaze met hers.

Alice bolted.

Chapter Fifteen

Axel cursed. When it rained, it poured. He'd finally gotten his mate in his territory and suddenly he had three of his pride members in his home. They weren't to blame, his home was the general headquarters for the pride, but damn, they were never here. He'd been there the day before and the house had been empty.

To make matters worse, Scarlet had broken the bad news to him that the hyenas had changed the location of the art piece they'd been after, so all their hard work had been for nothing. Then, he'd realized Ariadna wasn't with them and that's when he'd run, and just in time too. If he hadn't, God knew what would have happened. He didn't imagine she'd hurt Alice, but she would have scared her more than she already was. His mate had fled and now he was running after her and about to pounce because his lion was on the chase. It wasn't a question of common sense, it had become a question of pride and possession. She was his—his mate—and everyone had to know it so no one would ever dare question her again. Alice reached the end of the hallway and fumbled with the lock. He pounced. His animal instincts took over and he bit the top of her shoulder. She screamed and lost consciousness. He lapped at her blood and the wound disappeared. She was his. Finally. He roared his approval. Now all that was needed to complete the ritual was for them to mate carnally and for her to bite him. She would never truly be a lion, but she'd grow stronger, bolder. He shifted back into human form and picked her up in his arms, cradling her. And as he turned around, he caught sight of Ariadna still on her knees.

"Get out of here, Ariadna" he rumbled. "I can't deal with you right now."

Heading upstairs, he entered his bedroom and lay his mate on his—no, *their*—bed. Now all that was his would be hers. Pleasure coursed through him. He wanted to peel back the layers of her clothing, but he couldn't, not yet. They had to talk first, or she'd lose her mind. Things hadn't gone the way he'd wanted, but this could wait. This he would make sure would work out. He grabbed his robe and sat on the armchair at the foot of his bed. He waited.

It didn't take long before she started stirring. With a gasp she sat upright. She touched her shoulder and winced. She glanced at it. The shirt had ripped but there was nothing there, the spot where he'd pierced her gone when he'd lapped the blood.

"It will hurt for a few days."

"You bit me," she wept. Axel stood up to comfort her. She raised her hands with palms outward. "Get away from me."

She curled her knees to her chest and he returned to his position. He waited for her to speak. He'd already fucked up enough as it was. Finally, after a few tense minutes, she glanced at him.

"What have you done to me?"

He was going to explain but something in her voice stopped him.

"What do you mean?" he asked instead.

"I…" She shook her head. "This is embarrassing," she muttered.

"Baby Girl."

She bit her lip.

"I want you. I mean, I wanted you before, obviously, or I wouldn't have come here, but now, I just want to—" She fell silent.

"You want to what?"

"It's wrong. You attacked me."

"Tell me, Baby Girl," he demanded

Her cheeks flushed as their gazes locked.

"I want to fuck you. I'm burning inside. It's as if my skin were an incessant fire and all I want to do is strip and feel your hands on my body."

"Do it."

"What?"

"You heard me."

"You bit me," she said weakly.

"I did." He agreed. "But your desire hasn't lessened."

"Did you drug me?"

"No."

"Did you—"

"Alice," he interrupted her. "You said you wanted to take off your clothes and feel me. Stop thinking. Stop talking. Do what your body desires. Follow its order. Do it. Now."

VOLUME FOUR

Chapter Sixteen

Alice.

His voice struck a chord deep within her. She didn't know what it was, but the way he said her name was commanding yet full of warmth. It was stern, brooking no argument.

"Do it now. Don't make me repeat myself," he said in a low tone which sent a shiver across her spine.

Her cheeks were warm and probably red, but she was compelled to follow his order. *Do it now.* She wanted him. Badly. She had wanted him before but now it was a feverish pitch. Her pussy was wet and her nipples hard and aching. The only way to get rid of the ache was to have him. She didn't know why but she also didn't want to think more. She was tired of questioning everything. Exhausted from fearing everything around her. Being with Axel felt right.

All she had to do was follow his order. It was easy. She unbuttoned her shirt with trembling fingers. His heated stare had her nervous and aroused. She crept to the edge of the bed and clumsily took off her shoes and jeans. Part of her wanted to strip slowly, to make a show for him, but she couldn't bring herself to do it. She didn't even dare look at him.

"Come closer, Baby Girl."

Her heart stuck in her throat. She edged toward him, her heartbeat so loud it drowned all other sounds. She stopped a few feet from the chair.

"Closer."

She took another two small steps.

"Kneel."

Alice stooped, still without looking at him. When he grasped her chin and tilted her gaze upward, she gasped loudly. She hadn't heard him move, yet here he was standing in front of her, partially naked, the bulge under his robe very visible. Her mouth watered and she swallowed hard. Every inch of her engulfed in the flame of desire, which licked at her skin incessantly.

"Good girl."

A moan escaped her lips, drawing a grin from Axel. His gaze narrowed predatorily.

"What do you want, Baby Girl?"

Her gaze automatically flickered to his dick. He chuckled.

"Say it," he ordered. "I want to hear you vocalize your desire, Baby Girl."

"I-I want…" Alice swallowed. She shifted uncomfortably, sweat beading on her forehead.

"Your cock," he encouraged.

"Your cock," she repeated almost breathlessly.

"Where?" he asked while opening his robe and revealing the most perfect dick she'd ever seen. It curved upward, thick and glistening with pre-cum, the mushroom head both mesmerizing and enticing.

"Everywhere," she mumbled.

"In your mouth?"

"Yes." She bit her bottom lip, battling the urge to lean forward and kiss the bulbous tip.

"In your pussy?"

"Yes," she gasped, picturing it entering her, spreading her wide and filling her.

"In your ass?"

She hesitated.

"Yes," she finally said, glancing up at him. "Everywhere."

"Good girl, Baby Girl. You've earned a prize for your honesty." Axel took a step closer and placed the head of his engorged cock on her lips. "Open wide, Baby

Girl. Take what is yours."

She moaned as he slid into her. Her tongue arched upward, licking the thick vein at the length of his cock.

"Fuck, that's nice," he growled, pulling back and forth a few times. She made to grasp him, but he gripped her wrists, holding them over her head. Again and again, he thrust into her mouth. Saliva dribbled down her chin. Desire clawed at her skin, leaving an ache which demanded to be satisfied. Finally, Axel stepped back and released her.

"Did you like it, Baby Girl?" he asked, while massaging her arms.

"Yes…" Alice hesitated. The word *Daddy* rested on her lips. He'd asked her to call him that two days ago but now she faltered. Would it be okay? Wasn't it perverted? He was so much older. He could be her actual father. This wasn't right. Was it?

"Stop thinking," Axel demanded, tugging at her hair sharply. She gasped as pain mingled with pleasure. He didn't give her a chance to regain her bearings as his cock reentered her. Pleasure burst across her cells, and she moaned around his thickness. Her eyes watered as he fucked her mouth, slowly and then faster. Liquid coated the inside of her thighs, her pussy pulsing with every push and shove. *More.*

She wanted more. All other thoughts evaporated. Time stopped. Axel pulled her hair, pinpricks of pain traveled across her flesh. All that was left was them. Here at this moment. His hot rod in her, their scents of arousal mingling in the room. He groaned. She whimpered.

Desire. Pleasure. Pain.

More.

VOLUME FOUR

Chapter Seventeen

He couldn't read her mind, but he could take a good guess at what she had been thinking earlier. They had a twenty-year age difference. People would frown upon their relationship. Calling him Daddy was strange. Improper. None of it was important. She had to understand, all that mattered was them, what they believed, what they felt. The love, passion, and commitment they shared when they were together.

Axel groaned as she licked the head of his dick once more. Right now, the only thing that counted was their pleasure. He had to be inside of her. He pulled out his cock and flipped her around. Roughly, he pushed her against the bed and spread her legs. His digits slid into her pussy effortlessly.

"Fuck, you're slick, Baby Girl," he said. "Is this for me?"

"Yes, Daddy," the words came out like a desperate whimper. His heart skipped a beat, echoing the pounding of his cock.

"Baby Girl, I'm going to fuck you so hard."

Grasping her hips, he entered her in one full thrust. Alice ached her back and mewled in pleasure. Axel pulled back, using all his restraint, he kept his dick at her entrance. He grasped her hair again, turning her head slightly so she'd make eye contact with him.

"What do you want?" he asked.

"Fuck me."

"Excuse me?" he growled.

A slow, sexy grin spread across her lips. She wiggled her hips, forcing him to penetrate her further. Axel spanked her left ass cheek, and she yelped. Her smile grew broader.

"Fuck me, Daddy," she said.

With a triumphant growl, he flipped her on her back and lifted her legs to his shoulders. He pushed into her without preamble, pumping hard. Alice cried out with pleasure. She grabbed his biceps for balance. Their gazes locked. Her eyes were wide, pupils dilated as if she couldn't believe the pleasure coursing through her.

Axel ripped off her bra and bowed his head to suckle her breast. She gasped loudly. Quickly, he switched to the other one. He drove into her faster, her cries gaining a fevered pitch. Suddenly, Alice yelled out his name. Her orgasm washed over his dick, the contractions fueling his own passion.

"You're mine," he roared. With great effort he pulled back, his cum spewing between her legs and lower abdomen.

Alice didn't move, clearly still relishing her orgasms. Gently he lowered her legs and went into the en-suite bathroom. He returned with a damp towel and wiped away his semen.

"You'll come inside of me next time," she whispered.

He cocked his head, somewhat shocked by the brazen statement.

"Is that what you want?"

She nodded.

"Use your words."

"Yes." She opened her eyes and locked her gaze with his. "Daddy."

Chapter Eighteen

The words came out of her mouth with ease. Alice couldn't explain it, nor did she want to. For the first time in her life, she had stopped overthinking. It would come back, she didn't doubt it, but being here with Axel, in this moment, had been beyond anything she'd ever experienced. All she wanted to do was feel this way forever—hot, unconcerned for the past, present, or future, and yet cared for, wanted. Giving herself up to Axel had been a relief. The heated desire she'd experienced earlier was gone, replaced by a steady appetite only he could appease. She craved more. Fully. She wanted his dick pulsing inside of her as he orgasmed.

"Are you on oral contraception? Are you ready for children?"

"I, uh…" She gawked at him as reality came crashing back. Children? *No.* Axel was still a stranger. "No."

"We'll use condoms for the time being and we can see about oral—"

"No," she repeated.

His brow furrowed in confusion.

"Alice."

She touched her shoulder, which was still tender from his bite.

"I … this is insanity, Axel. You attacked me. I don't know what you've done to me." She scurried away from the bed, fishing out her clothes.

"Alice, stop."

She ignored him and tried to put on her bra realizing it was broken. Tears threatened the corner of her eyes. She was a nutcase. One second, she was living the moment and the next everything spiraled out of control.

"Alice." Axel grabbed her by the upper arms and forced her to stand in front of him. "Baby Girl. You are my mate."

Alice blinked. The words penetrated her mind. *You are my mate.* She recalled what Ariadna had said earlier. *"Life mates are destined to be together. They are bound to one lover for life, and they can immediately recognize the person that completes them, the person who will lighten up their world."*

"Excuse me," she said.

Axel sighed. "This is not how I wanted it to go at all," he muttered. "Come." He led her to the armchair and sat down, pulling her onto his lap. Alice didn't fight him. She waited, breath abated, her heart pulsing wildly. *Mates?*

"Shifters have mates," Axel said. "The person who becomes their one and only. Once we meet our mates, our animal knows there is no one else out there for us, but for the mating to be complete I had to bite you. I didn't want the other women to question you or who you are to me."

"Bite?"

"But there is more," he plunged on. "You must bite me too. You have to mark me to make the mating complete."

"What?" Alice gaped at him. Questions and incoherent thoughts tumbled across her tongue, piling in her mind.

"I don't get it," she finally said. "The woman earlier, Ariadna, said she was your mate. Can you have more than one?"

"Ariadna is not my mate," Axel said sternly. "She has always wanted a position of power in the pride. I believe she recognized you as my lover and she became jealous. I am not pleased with her behavior."

"So, she's not your girlfriend? "

"There's no one but you, Alice."

"Will I become a shifter?" she asked.

"No." Axel brushed a strand of hair behind her ear. Alice shivered. "Once the mating is complete you might become a bit stronger, or faster, but nothing else."

"Oh." She hesitated. "What if I refuse?"

Axel stared at her in silence for what seemed like hours. He seemed to be measuring his words. Finally, he spoke. "If you refuse, we will both be miserable forever. There will be no one else for either of us. Ever."

"So, I'm bound to you, whether I want it or not."

He nodded. "Do you think that is a bad thing?" He squeezed her thigh sending a jolt of erotic electricity through her system. Alice shook her head.

"The sex is great, but I don't know you, and you don't know me. I never thought, I mean I always thought I'd meet someone and eventually after many dates we'd fall in love, get married. You know, the usual."

"I understand. We shifters like to cut to the chase. We are in a way animals, and human games are a waste of time. Nonetheless," he said with a smile, "My intention was to court you, but things have turned out differently. I don't regret it. Do you?"

Alice gazed into his eyes. They were the color of amber, she decided. They were full of kindness, and a fire deep within she could not escape. She gave a brief nod.

"No," she finally said. "But I'm afraid."

"That is normal, Baby Girl. Trust me when I tell you I won't let anything bad happen to you." Axel took a deep breath. "And you don't need to mate with me yet. I want you to," he added, "but I understand if you want to wait to get to know me a bit better."

Alice let out a sigh of relief.

"Thanks. I appreciate it." She bit her lip nervously

and shifted on his lap. "Daddy." Her eyes widened as she noticed the rise of his erection under her butt.

Axel grinned mischievously. "Of course, Baby Girl." He slid his index fingertip across her chest, over the rise of her breasts. Her breath caught. "Now, though, I'm not letting you out of this room until we're both fully sated."

Chapter Nineteen

Alice woke up. She really needed to pee. She glanced at Axel and a smile flitted over her lips. He was sound asleep. How many times had she orgasmed? She shook her head, pushing the erotic thoughts aside, and slowly got out of bed.

After making use of the bathroom, she put on one of the robes behind the door and slowly headed downstairs, while rolling up the burgundy sleeves. Sunlight streamed from large floor-to-ceiling windows at the top of the staircase, illuminating the entire foyer. What time was it?

As soon as she reached the bottom floor, her feet landing on the cold marble, Alice regretted her decision. What if Ariadna decided to chase after her again? Or one of the others? Axel has said there were three lionesses in the house. She'd met two. She glanced back the way she'd come. There could also be other lions. He'd explained during the night the house was the place where the lions gathered. Axel normally lived in the city, but his house was being renovated, and this is where they came to hang out and run in freedom.

Alice swallowed. She was thirsty and hungry. She glanced through one of the arches. She could do this. Axel had promised they wouldn't hurt her, and she believed him, right? She made her way through one of the hallways. Surely, the kitchen had to be this way, right? She could smell coffee being brewed.

The smell became stronger as she approached a set of wooden doors left open. Whispers could be heard coming from within. She froze, but it was too late, they had already seen her. Three women stood around the kitchen island, chatting amiably in pajamas. They looked at her, surprise also clear on their faces.

"I'm sorry," she murmured, backing up.

"No, wait," Ariadna spoke up. "Please, don't leave." She hurried forward, her hands steepled in a plea. "I want to apologize."

"You do?"

Alice hesitated.

"Yes. I acted out of … well, I was … I have always wanted—"

"To be queen," Scarlet piped in. She came around, stood behind Alice, draped an arm across her shoulders, and began to lead her back to the kitchen.

Ariadna scowled for an instant, then her features dropped.

"Yes." She sighed. "I had been hoping maybe one day Axel's lion would take me as its mate, and when I saw you, well, I could smell him on you, and I acted like an idiot."

"You really don't have to apologize."

"Of course I do," Ariadna said. She smiled slyly. "You have *almost* mated. Once you realize you have no escape, you will mate him, and you will become family. I don't want us to hate each other, it would make family functions quite difficult to bear." She chuckled, drily.

"We must respect you," the third woman said. She was also blonde, but unlike the other two, her eyes were green, and she had a piercing on her bottom lip and eyebrow. "I'm Bea, by the way. I was out running when this whole fiasco happened." She moved toward Alice with her hand extended. Alice took it politely.

"I am a stranger," Alice said. "I wouldn't dare demand anything."

"You don't need to. We are in part animals and the laws by which we play are very strict. We respect those above us in the hierarchy, until the day we have our own pride, if ever," Scarlet said.

"I'm sorry," Alice said. "I didn't ask for any of this. I'll gladly—"

"Nonsense. It's great to have another woman in the family. We are the true leaders," Scarlet said, beckoning her closer to the table. "Would you like some coffee?"

Alice nodded.

"Why don't you tell us a bit about yourself, Alice?" Bea asked.

Alice's stomach knotted at the unexpected question. Her innards squeezed painfully as her mind aimed to find something to say. She was once more saved by Scarlet.

"Would you like some milk or sugar?"

"Both, please," she said eagerly.

Bea and Ariadna both laughed.

"You must really need that java. Where are you from? What do you do? How long have you known Axel?"

Alice blanched.

"I'm from, em, New York, born and raised in the suburbs," she managed to say.

Thick and oppressive silence crept around her as she didn't offer any more information. What was she supposed to say? Was it her turn to ask questions? Weren't they being too inquisitive? Alice's knot tripled in size, becoming almost unbearable. Her heart pounded frantically.

"I'm not very good at small talk," she blurted.

"Sometimes all you need is a bit of practice," Scarlet said, handing her a steaming mug.

"That's what my therapist says," she mumbled.

Ariadna laughed.

"Scarlet is a therapist."

"Oh." Alice glanced at the woman, who winked at her. Was that why she was being so helpful? Did she realize her struggle?

"Let's take it one step at a time. We don't need to know everything right now."

Alice took a sip of her coffee. She let out a long sigh. These women were just trying to be friendly. She recalled her own therapist's words. You can't assume everyone is out to get you, Alice.

"I work in finance right now, for PAM," she said.

"Oh," Bea said. Abruptly, she hastily began to fold the papers which had been strewn on the table. One of them slipped to the floor and Alice bent to pick it up. Her brow wrinkled as she recognized the image.

"Wait," she said. "I know this office. It's my boss's office."

"What?" all three women exclaimed in unison.

Scarlet carefully plucked the photograph from her hands. "Alice, has Axel told you what else we do here?" she asked, caution lacing her words.

"No," Alice replied quietly, a sense of foreboding prickling her scalp unpleasantly.

Chapter Twenty

Alice hurried back upstairs. The woman had refused to explain anything, so she'd left her coffee on the counter and headed to see Axel. In her mind a whirlwind of questions formed.

Why did they have a picture of her boss's office? What were the rest of the papers they had stowed away? What other job did Axel have besides the bar?

Lost in her thoughts, she crashed into Axel just as he left the bedroom.

"Hey, Baby Girl." His smile changed to a frown. "What's going on?"

"Why do you have a picture of my boss's office?" she asked without preamble.

"What?"

"I saw it now, downstairs. The girls say you must tell me what else you do for a living. What is it?"

Axel pressed his lips together. He ran his fingers through his hair.

"All right. Relax, Baby Girl. I can explain."

"Then do it. Do it now. Why the secretiveness?" She tugged the lapels of his robe. Fear slithered its ugly head around her neck. What was he hiding?

"I'm an art thief. We're art thieves," Axel said.

Her hands dropped. She took a step back.

"Excuse me?"

Axel sighed.

"That's how I've made my fortune. I'm a stealthy cat. We steal art for rich people who want peculiar paintings."

"And what does my boss's office have to do with any of this?"

"The painting in your CEO's office is the one my

latest client wants."

"So, you're going to steal it? Have you … is this—you and I—because you want to access the building? Am I just a pawn in this heist?"

She crossed her arms to her chest, fighting off the shivers which threatened to wrack her frame.

"God, no! No, Alice. You just happen to work in the same place, but it has nothing to do with us. We have a picture of all the offices with accessible windows. That's all. Your boss's office has a window, which would make it easier for us to enter, that's it."

"It's on the second floor, how are you going to climb to the second floor? What you're saying doesn't make sense."

"Alice, there's a fire escape ladder. Trust me. We've done this before."

"How often? Never mind, don't answer. Your fortune is dirty money."

"Alice, please, we steal from the rich for the rich. We're not taking anything from people like you or your friends."

"No." She put her hands up, staving him away. "No. I'm sorry, Axel. This is too much. Lion shifters and now this. Thieves. You're all freaking thieves. I thought I could deal with the shifting aspect, if it's even real. At this point, I'm not sure if this is some kind of drug-induced dream, but thievery? You're like the mob. No. I'm done. I'm leaving."

She marched past him to grab her clothes. She quickly began to get dressed in jerky movements.

"Alice."

"Don't touch me." She snatched her arm from Axel's soft grip.

"I understand. I've pushed you too far, Baby Girl, in too short a time. I'll drive you home."

"No. I'll call an Uber or a cab. I want you, no, scratch that, I *need* you to stay away from me." She shook her head. "I can't think clearly when you're around, Axel."

"No Uber will take you into the city from here. This isn't easy to find, and besides, it's expensive. Let me drive you."

"No."

"Fine," he growled. "Then, I'll ask one of the girls to take you. Please, Alice."

Alice clenched her jaw to hide the tremble within her. She didn't think he was lying when he said an Uber wouldn't take her back into the city. She couldn't recall how long it had taken them to drive out here. Yesterday, it had all been a sweet dream. Today, reality came crashing all around her, breaking perfection into tiny shards of glass which cut deeply. She didn't know where she was, and she clearly didn't know who this man was. She needed to leave before she got hurt more.

"Fine. Just get me out of here," she said.

VOLUME FOUR

Chapter Twenty-One

Alice glanced out the window. The countryside rolled by ablaze in red, orange, and yellow woodlands. Absently, she wondered how Axel managed to maintain his place, looking like a savannah when all around him were pines, maples, and oaks.

Axel.

Her insides twisted painfully. This time, though, it wasn't the knot in her stomach, a new one had formed in her heart, and she couldn't push it away. It squeezed with every breath, stealing her focus and forcing a keening sadness to the forefront. She would never see him again.

Daddy. Axel.

Frustrated, she wiped away a tear. How could she be crying over something which had never come to be? This had all been a mistake, a dream brought on by her own tendencies to make a mountain out of an anthill. She was weak. A mess of a person.

"Are you okay?" Scarlet asked, startling her.

"What do you think?" she snapped. "I'm sorry, I didn't mean to be so rude. Thank you for driving me."

"No need to apologize, Alice. It's a lot to take in, in such a short amount of time. I would be freaking out as well if I were you."

"But you're not me."

"Of course not." Scarlet glanced at her then focused on the road once more. "I was brought up in this world. I know what it's like and how hard it is to survive. Being a shifter is not something we choose."

"I can imagine."

"Axel didn't ask—"

"I'm not leaving because he's a shifter," she explained.

Scarlet sucked in her cheeks before speaking up again.

"Why then?" she asked.

"You're thieves. Robbers. It's immoral. I should probably call the police on you, if I had any proof." Alice dug her fingers into her knees. For some reason, calling the woman who was driving her home and being incredibly kind to her a thief, made her sick to her stomach.

"We do what we have to do to maintain our lifestyle. We're not hurting anyone."

"What about the people you're stealing from?"

"Alice, we're not stealing from people like you. We're not stealing from the average worker. We're robbing artwork from people who have too much money to begin with. They are people who don't know what to do with their fortune, and we're being paid by the same people. It's a game for them, see who has the best art piece regardless of the price."

"It's still not an excuse."

"It's not," Scarlet agreed. "I'm just trying to make you see where we come from. You know," she said. "Axel and I were college buddies. He got into the business way before I did. He'll tell you himself, but his first jobs weren't art, they were university exams and such. Then books, and eventually art. Word spread around campus. I also needed money, so I sought him out and joined him. We were two lion shifters who had to pay our way through school."

"What about your parents?"

Scarlet scoffed. "He comes from a line of purist shifters. They set him free and on his feet, as soon as he turned eighteen. He had to find his own way in life."

"And you? As soon as my parents discovered I'd met a lion who was starting their own pride, they cut the cord."

"That's harsh."

"It is the way of the lion." Scarlet shrugged.

"It shouldn't be. You're telling me that if I were to have children with Axel, I'd have to give them up when they turned eighteen? Are you crazy? You're a mother for life."

"I couldn't agree more, but this is something you'd have to bring up with Axel. Mixed couples are different. Ariadna's parents are mixed. She is a shifter, but her brother is not. Her parents are loving and doting on both children. They do not, however, belong to a pride. They decided to focus on their more human side. So, as you see, it depends on what you choose to do with your mate."

"I see." Alice looked out the window once more. What future would she have with Axel when they had children? She wouldn't be willing to give them up because of some stupid pride rule. Alice grimaced. Why on earth was she entertaining these thoughts? Children? She was leaving Axel forever. He was a stranger. There was no future if there'd never even been a present. Her heart seemed to disagree, clutching painfully and leaving her almost breathless.

"In any case," Alice said. "I was taught stealing is wrong, so I'll stick to that. Besides, this whole mating thing is too complicated. I am anxious, you know? I can't deal with any of it. It's too much. I need peace and calm, and a slow, measured approach to things."

Scarlet nodded.

"I understand. Don't worry." She gave her a soft smile. "Although, life has a habit of biting us in the ass."

"That's not very encouraging coming from a psychologist," Alice retorted. For some reason, Scarlet's words angered her, just as when her therapist had pointed out some of her flaws were her own doing.

She laughed heartily.

"That was a piece of friendly advice, not coming from a therapist."

Chapter Twenty-Two

Axel watched Alice get in the car and leave. He hoped with all his heart she'd look back, but she didn't. Desperation clawed within him. His lion dug its claws into his chest, and he grimaced. Pain unlike anything he'd known before twisted his innards. He didn't realize he was shifting until it was too late. His clothes ripped and tumbled to the floor. He set after them at a run.

Alice.

He picked up his pace, roaring her name in a frantic plea. "*Alice!*"

His heart hammered her name in his chest and mind. She couldn't leave him. She was his mate. His one and only. After forty years he'd finally found her and now she was driving away, leaving him forever. She couldn't.

Scarlet must have spotted him because she stepped on the accelerator and the car sped forward. His paws hit the asphalt, the hard cold ground burning them as he sped up. He would run all the way to the city. He would catch up with them and drag Alice back home with him. *Baby Girl.*

The car turned a bend, and he lost them from his sight for an instant. It was enough to bring him back to his wits. He slowed down, easing into a softer gait. His breath came out in short spurts. Tension ebbed from his shoulders. His limbs turned heavy. Grief embraced him in a heavy hug, and he shifted back into his human form. He fell to his knees.

Come back, please.

Throughout his life he'd made many mistakes, but he'd never messed up so badly as he had now. Somehow, he had managed to conquer and lose his mate in less than twenty-four hours.

He covered his face in desperation. Reality struck him across his back like a belt whipped at him. He yelled out his frustration. He knew even if he had caught up with the vehicle, he'd never be able to bring Alice back with him forcefully. She'd hate him and they'd be miserable forever.

No. Even though the animal within him was whimpering in despair, he had to think reasonably. It was time for the human to take charge. Slowly, he got to his feet. Alice needed time. They would both benefit from a few days away from each other. He would come up with a new plan to win her over. After all, he was a hunter, and he would not so easily give up on his prey.

Chapter Twenty-Three

Alice sat down at her desk with a sigh. Her boss walked by, his face clouded with disapproval as he glanced in her direction. She lowered her head, pretending to work at her computer but once again her mind was elsewhere.

Ever since she'd left Axel, her life had been miserable. At the office, her boss gave her an evil stare every other day, as if he knew she was planning something against him, and she ran behind in her work.

At home, Nessa kept pestering her for information on what had happened to the hunk. Once she'd told him they'd stopped seeing each other after a night of passion, she'd turned to praise her for leaving him and scolding her for going to his house without telling anyone where she was.

She'd tried to see her therapist, but her next appointment wasn't until next week, so she was left alone with her thoughts, which had been a nightmare.

One whole week. Alice wasn't even sure how she'd managed to survive. Whenever she wasn't working or pretending to do so, she was thinking about Axel. She forgot mealtimes, shower times, and bedtime. All she could manage was to conjure Axel's picture. She masturbated to him, the need to do so every night becoming imperative, then she would cry herself to sleep, recalling and missing his warmth and loving embrace.

It was insanity. Ridiculous. She tried to convince herself it had only been a one-night stand. Tons of people had one every day and they didn't become obsessed with each other. Had she had the best sex in her life? Yes. But that was it. She didn't know Axel. He was not a bar owner, he was a gangster, a thief. She was certain when she told her therapist, they'd laugh about it. Right?

"Alice?"

She lifted her gaze, surprised to find her boss standing in front of her desk, grinning at her unpleasantly. For some reason, Kenneth had always reminded her of a hyena. His smile was too wide and toothy. He was tall and lean, with angular features, a strong jawline and a flat wide nose, upturned at the tip. His dark hair was constantly tousled, as if he couldn't stop running his fingers through it.

"Yes?" she said.

"Before you leave today, please come into my office. I'd like to have a word with you."

Dread wound its way into her, coiling into a lead ball.

"Of course," she managed to say.

Shit.

It was just what she needed. Her love life was in shambles, and now she was surely going to get fired. It was true that her work hadn't been the best this week. She'd almost turned in a report late, but she'd stayed up all night finishing it and had successfully sent it.

Alice forced herself to focus on her work. She had to make it through the rest of the afternoon. She glanced at the clock. One more hour.

Finally, people began to leave. She waved goodbye to a few coworkers and stood up. Her legs shook. Taking a deep breath, she made her way to Kenneth's office. Unable to help it, her gaze landed on the window Axel had told her about. They were on the second floor. Sure, he could access through that window, but then what? They had to make it all the way to the top to the CEO's office on the twelfth floor. There was security throughout the building. It was suicidal no matter what he'd said.

"Alice." Kenneth greeted her with another one of his characteristic smiles, sending a shiver down her back. "Close the door and have a seat."

Nervously, she obeyed. As soon as she sat down, Kenneth leaned forward, folding his hands atop his desk and creating a steeple. His dark gaze met hers.

"Alice, your work this week hasn't been up to standards. You were hired after your one-year internship because we thought you were promising."

"I'm sorry. It's been a rough week. I promise I'll do better."

"Let me finish." Alice stared at her lap, cheeks burning. "I'm afraid you will not continue to work here, Alice."

"Why? Surely, you're not firing me because of a bad week."

"No. I'm firing you because you reek of lion."

"What?" Her jaw dropped in shock.

"You heard me. Did you think we wouldn't notice? You've been with the lions. You smell of them, and unfortunately, we are not on the best terms with those sneaky cats."

"We? Who are *we*? You're firing me because I smell like a lion? I'm not a shifter," she cried. "This is madness." She held her head, overwhelmed with despair.

"It doesn't matter. You've been too close to them. Our alliances here at PAM lie with other shifters. Please gather your things and don't come back tomorrow."

Alice stared at Kenneth. His eyes were devoid of emotion. In a dreamlike state, she stood up and crossed the room. She glanced back one last time, wishing for all of this to be a joke, but Kenneth was already back at work.

Fighting the onset of tears, she collected her few belongings and headed outside. As soon as the cool air slapped her in the face, the tears rolled. Almost blindly, she made her way across the street. It wasn't until she realized where she was that she stopped.

She took in THE GIN ROOM sign. The gold lettering and the soft yellow glow beckoned to her. Why had she made her way here of all places?

Axel might be in there. He would comfort her. Except, he was just as twisted as her boss. No, she had to find her own way in life. Wiping away the tears, she bowed her head and continued to the subway.

She never made it.

Chapter Twenty-Four

Axel hung up. Panic threatened to consume him, but he pushed it down with a hard shove. Right now, he had to act. There was no time for misery. They had Alice. He had to get her back no matter what.

He glanced at his phone. He didn't want to get the rest of the pride involved. They were after him, he had no doubt, or they wouldn't have taken Alice. No, he knew exactly what he had to do.

An hour later, as they'd instructed, he arrived at Alice's office. He pushed through the building doors, finding them open, just as they'd told him they'd be. In one glance, he took in the space around him. A reception desk to one side, empty. Entrance turnstiles for employees to clock in, and after them a set of elevators which would take them to their place of work. He took one of them and pressed the button for the top floor. The CEO's office.

The doors opened into the office. Floor-to-ceiling windows stretched along the back, giving an impressive view of the city skyline. The desk, situated in front of the windows, commanded attention with its sleek glass surface and polished edges. Behind it, a man sat motionless, flanked by two large, muscular men dressed in dark suits.

To the sides of the room, several paintings adorned the walls—the one they had been planning to steal back in its place. Diplomas and certificates framed in gold added an air of authority, while shelves filled with trophies and books showcased the owner's knowledge. Next to one of these, a closed door.

None of the figures caught his attention. The only thing that mattered was the woman sitting on the brown leather couch. Alice. Her hands and feet were bound, and her posture was rigid with fear. Red-rimmed eyes locked onto his. Her bottom lip trembled as she mouthed his name.

He went to her, kneeled, and undid her bonds.

"You okay, Baby Girl?" He cupped her chin, brushing the stray tear aside with the pad of his thumb.

"Yes, but Axel—"

"I'm sorry to interrupt this tender scene, but Axel, I believe we have business to discuss."

Axel stood up and turned his attention to the man at the desk. CEO Alastair Jubatus saluted him with a nod and sly smile. Even though he was not tall, Alastair had a muscular build, though his most striking feature were his piercing green eyes and high cheekbones.

"Alastair Jubatus. I would say it is a pleasure to see you again, but since your father's death and our brief meeting then, I haven't had the pleasure."

The cheetah shifter's gaze narrowed.

"How is the coalition?" Axel asked. "Last I heard, you were struggling to maintain the cheetahs together, but I see now you've allied with the hyenas. A bold move."

"Not as bold as you attempting to steal from me," Alastair said.

Axel chuckled.

"Thank you. I do relish a challenge."

Alastair clasped his hands over his desk.

"At the cost of your mate?" he asked, raising an eyebrow.

"She came along for the ride after I'd accepted the job."

"Yes, which is why you made a set of mistakes which have brought you here tonight. You see, Axel, there never really was a painting for you to steal."

Alastair stood up and began making his way

throughout the room to the empty spot on the wall. "Let me explain myself. Initially, there was a painting. My good friend, your new client, C.C., wanted this masterpiece, but when I learned I could completely eradicate you and your pride from my turf, things changed. I decided to gift C.C. the painting so he wouldn't have to steal it, and paid for his silence."

"So, you want to get rid of my pride? You realize there are other lion shifters in New York, right?"

"Of course, but you're the ones in my area, my neighborhood, so to speak. Everyone knew about the Collector's Pride. You are well known for your work, Axel, that was not an issue. The problem came when you opened that bar, The Gin Room. Your presence became too close for comfort. One moment you're dealing with art, and the next you're getting under my nose, you know what I mean?"

Axel looked at Alastair with incredulity.

"You're telling me that instead of coming to talk to me personally, you decided to kidnap my mate and force me to come here. I have my own business, I would never meddle in yours. This jealousy and cock show is unnecessary. For fuck's sake, Alastair, your father would never approve."

"Stop bringing up my father, Alastair snapped. "He's dead."

"Yes, and he was my friend, and he agreed to me opening that bar. What do you think, kid? I just waltzed in here and decided to set up a business? I know my stuff."

"Well, Axel, I don't think you do because if you did, you would have realized you were walking right into a trap, and when my mate found out who yours was, well, it was as if destiny was handing me your head on a silver platter."

"Your mate?"

"Nessa, come out."

At that moment, a woman peeked her head through the adjacent door.

"Come, darling, time to reveal your face."

Axel gaped and started to laugh.

"Nessa?" Alice cried.

"Sorry, Alice. I tried to warn you, but you wouldn't listen," Nessa said. She took Alastair's hand. "This was the guy I was telling you about the other night."

Axel growled low. He could hear Alice's heartbeat and labored breathing. She was not doing well. It was time to cut to the chase.

"All right, Alastair, so what do you want? For us to close the bar and leave?"

"Initially, yes, but now that I have you here, I want your head, Axel. If we get rid of you, not only will the bar be closed but your little pride will come down like a pack of dominoes. It would be one less thing to worry about, one less rival to watch out for. The hyenas could dominate the art industry with the cheetahs at their side."

Axel rubbed his temples.

"Alastair, I couldn't care less about your little gang war, but I'll tell you what. Let me help my mate. Give me your word she'll get out of here safely and we'll fight, though your father is probably stirring in his grave, but you need a lesson."

"No!" Alice screamed.

He shot her a warning glance. Alastair chuckled and rubbed his hands together.

"Fair enough. I wouldn't want you to harm mine anyway." He winked at Nessa, who blushed. "The two of them can leave. Nessa, honey, get out of here."

"No," Alice wept running into his arms. Axel

embraced her. He clasped her chin and forced her gaze to his.

"Trust me," he said. "Everything is going to be okay." He clasped her right hand. "Do you feel the strength of my fingers? Every joint, every callous. Stay grounded, Baby Girl. You'll be holding it again in no time. I promise."

"Axel, please."

Nessa grabbed Alice's forearm and pulled her away from him. Axel turned his attention back to Alastair. As soon as he heard the elevator ping shut, he grinned and stripped off his jacket.

"All right, kitty cat, let's teach you a lesson in diplomacy."

VOLUME FOUR

Chapter Twenty-Five

Alice pulled out of Nessa's grasp as soon as they reached the bottom. Pushing her out the doors, she hit the button for the last floor.

"Alice!" Nessa screamed. She tried to fight her way back in, but the elevator was already closing.

Alice gave her another hard shove, sending her sprawling onto the polished floor.

"I thought we were friends," she cried.

"Alice, please, don't be silly. Don't go back up there," Nessa yelled.

But it was too late, the box was moving steadily up. Her heart hammered in her ears and her breath came out in spurts, and black spots danced in her vision, but she fought against the panic. She had to do something. She had to help somehow. Axel was in danger.

The doors slid open with a chime. A scream caught in her throat at the ghastly sight, and she rushed forward. The two bodyguards which had kidnapped her saw her and hurried to restrain her. She fought against them, but it was useless. Wide-eyed, she watched the scene unfold.

Two wild animals clashed violently in the middle of the office. They broke apart, crashing into bookcases and sending the contents tumbling to the floor.

Clearly heavier and larger, the lion approached the cheetah in large strides, but the smaller animal darted to one side and then the other, its speed unsurpassable. Alastair evaded every move from Axel with an agility which was difficult to follow with the naked eye.

Without warning, it lashed out, cutting through the lion's flank with its claws. The lion roared in pain and pounced in retaliation, seizing the cheetah between in mid-stride. The cheetah struggled to get up, but the lion was too powerful, keeping it pinned down on the floor. It was over in minutes. The lion's superior weight and strength evident.

Eventually, the two men shifted back. Axel had Alastair pinned down, the younger man bleeding profusely from claw marks on his shoulders where he'd been held.

"This is why cheetahs don't mess with lions," Axel said with a growl. "I will not get in your way, Alastair. Don't you get in mine. Do the smart thing, build alliances, not enemies. When you're ready to talk, come see me."

Alastair nodded. Fear was etched on his face.

Axel released him and turned to her with a victorious smile. The bodyguards released her, and she ran to his arms, snuggling her face into his chest. She fought back the tears of relief.

"Thanks for waiting, Baby Girl." He grasped her hand and squeezed. "I told you you'd feel it again," he whispered in her ear.

She nodded.

"Are you okay?" he asked, twisting so he could look at her face.

"I'm fine. I was scared for you."

"You were brave. You are brave, Alice."

"Not enough. I—"

Axel smiled kindly.

"Let's get out of here and talk, Baby Girl."

Chapter Twenty-Six

Alice shifted nervously in her seat. She tried to keep herself from fidgeting in the black dress she wore. It had been the only thing she'd found in her closet that wasn't jeans and hoodies and nice enough to go out to one of the most expensive restaurants in the cities. The soft warm glow of the lights created an intimate ambience. The tables were placed so each diner had a sense of privacy, while the rich purple velvet chairs, a staple of the restaurant, combined perfectly with the rest of the high-end décor.

She took a sip of the wine they'd ordered, relishing the taste. She recalled the last hour of her life with a smile. As soon as they had stepped out of her workplace, Axel had crushed her in his arms and kissed her until she couldn't breathe. Then, he'd taken her hand and led her to his car. She'd tried to say something, to explain, but he'd told her to save it for later.

"I get extremely hungry after a fight, Baby Girl. We're going to your place to get you something nice to wear, as well as some essentials for the weekend, and then we're going out to dinner to The Velvet Parlor."

"But Axel."

"No, buts, Baby Girl. I need to eat so I can think and properly woo you."

"Axel, you don't need to woo me."

"Silence, or I'll spank your ass raw."

Too shocked to say much else, she'd kept quiet while he made some work calls. Back at her place, he'd helped her pack some things and waited while she showered and changed. Then they'd taken the car back here, and now he'd gone to the bathroom and left her alone with her thoughts.

The truth was, she was all over the place. On the one hand, the fight and the fear of losing him had made her see she couldn't live without him. She loved him, as crazy as that was. Being with Axel felt right. On the other hand, she was still terrified of the future. Now she was jobless, and thieving wasn't something she ever wanted to get into. Besides, her whole world had suddenly opened to an array of shifters which might not want her in it if they mated.

"A penny for your thoughts," Axel whispered in her ear, his warm breath and voice like a caress in her most intimate places.

"You'll get them for free, I'm afraid." She smiled nervously. Alice clenched and unclenched her hands, then clasped them together. Axel sat and covered them with his much larger ones. "Axel," she started.

"Tell me, Baby Girl."

She cocked her head in awe. How could his gaze devour her and at the same time peel back the layers of endless fear she covered herself with? She was naked under him, yet she was also safe. He wouldn't judge her.

"I love you," she blurted.

His pupils dilated with undeniable pleasure and a smile which melted her heart formed on his lips.

"And I love you, Baby Girl."

Alice breathed deeply, the knowledge of his feelings fueling her next words.

"But I'm scared about the mating. I don't think I can do it. Not yet. I need time," she said, the torrent of words spilling without pause.

"Alice, I will give you all the time you need. You have already gifted me with your love. What more could a man ask for?"

"You will?"

"As long as you're with me, Baby Girl, as long as

you love me, that is all that matters. We don't need to complete the mating ritual right now. The animal can wait. I am certain of our bond. We can wait until you're ready."

Tears gathered at the corner of her eye. She sniffed. Axel stood and kneeled in front of her.

"Ignore the rest of the people, Baby Girl. This is about you and me," he said soothingly, as if he understood the embarrassment the public display caused her. "I want you to know I will take care of you, Baby Girl. No matter what. I love you."

Alice focused on his eyes and his face. This was her mate. Her man. She wasn't ready to mate officially yet, but deep down she knew she'd take the step soon. She leaned forward and found Axel's lips. His small gasp of surprise making her giggle.

"I am yours, Daddy. Forever."

The End

VOLUME FOUR

FERAL MOON RISING

Monsters of New York

Raven Hush

Copyright © 2025

Chapter One

Gray

My best friend had an unhealthy sexual appetite that annoyed the shit out of me. I watched Blake grind himself against a half-undressed stripper on the VIP stage in the upstairs area of the Gin Room and prayed I wouldn't have to tow his drunk ass out the door by the end of the night.

Two weeks in New York City and I was already sick of babysitting his shifter ass, because according to the local panther claw we had linked up with out of necessity only, he couldn't be trusted to look after himself.

Not that it was news to me. Blake had been getting us both into shit since we tried to enroll in college together a decade ago. No surprises when that didn't turn out so well either. Shifters—especially ones who couldn't keep their claws or teeth to themselves—weren't popular items on a campus that wasn't supposed to know we existed.

A waiter paused by my chair where I sat slightly behind the blackout curtain and raised the bottle of Yamazaki single malt with no label—I'd taken a liking to it on my last visit. The elusive club owner's personal recommendation sat well with me. Evading local northern-state-based law enforcement didn't mean I had to give up luxuries I'd spent over fifteen years building in an attempt to keep Blake and I out of a scientist's laboratory.

Which was what would happen if we were caught with our literal pants down.

Shifters were a rumor at best, a nightmare the human population feared. There was plenty of evidence kept away under lock and key but the scant independent panther community wasn't organized enough to do anything about it. Tempers—including mine—were unpredictable in enclosed spaces. But that wasn't how we ended up leaving the safety of our extended, if somewhat uncommunicative, claw up North and leeching onto an overpopulated city, based on the one who took us in here. Safety in numbers and all, or at least that was how the local pseudo-alpha sold his package to us. Even as solitary hunters, most panther shifters knew we wouldn't survive long in this world if we traveled alone once we hit the glitz of city lights.

Which was a damn fine reason to stay the hell away from them.

If I had it my way, we'd stay in the Adirondacks, which was still my backup plan for when all this went to shit. Blake, I knew, had another destination in mind. We could draw straws after tonight. A quick glance at the stage told me we weren't far from that point.

Blake's skin rippled, dark shadows that preceded his change marling his otherwise tanned skin in whorls that moved with him. Chartreuse eyes turned to solid obsidian, and razored claws extended from his hands in lieu of fingernails.

"The fuck." I slammed the whiskey in its crystal tumbler onto the short table at my side, breaking the pure silence rule of the blackout section within the VIP area, and rose. My beast roiled against the cage of my chest, ready to shred the single silk blend suit I had left in my possession, but this was not the time to ruin it.

Humans were already afraid of us enough and though the bar, upper class as it may position itself, allowed shifters through the door, it did not condone a panther and human copulating onstage in clear view of others.

Nor did it seem the other dancer agreed as she fled the stage while her friend groped my best friend's fur-covered arms and writhed beneath him in an impromptu show of utter bullshit.

"He could get better on a porn channel," I spat.

The server who watched me with wide eyes backed off, clutching his prized bottle of whiskey.

I shook my head, striding to the stage, and took the ten-foot leap in one, landing in a crouch, hardly out of breath beside Blake. "Are you out of your goddamn mind? We left motherfucking Canada because of your shit. Now you start up again? We're gonna run out of borrowed claws and landmasses, my friend."

And I'll be out of patience.

Blake turned his blackened eyes on me, blinking them back to his normal pale green that reflected in most of our kind. I stood alone with gray eyes, hence the name. But before he shook his head, a flicker of something I didn't expect swirled around his pupils—a craze of purple that ringed the green, and then it was gone.

"The fuck," I muttered again, relegated to single syllables. I gripped Blake's nape, clamping my hand over his cheek and pushing his eyelids back, but the purple streak didn't make a second appearance. A heavy scent of a second unwelcome surprise, however, did. *Pheromones.* "You take something?" I released him and backed up a step, forgetting I was onstage and nearly fell off the damn thing.

"No." Blake rubbed his neck, shaking his head. "I … had a bit to drink. Sorry, sweetheart. Maybe another time." He gave her a watery version of his usually impish grin, brushing some of her lip gloss from her cheek that had his fur stuck in it.

I snorted. "Classy. Let's go."

"What? I'm good, bro," Blake protested.

I nodded, my back to him as I stepped off the ten-foot drop from the stage and landed on my feet, walking past the same server who still stared at me, the whites of his eyes showing.

Damn, that's gonna cost me.

I slipped a wad of notes out of my jacket pocket and tucked them onto his tray, not breaking the blackout section's complete silence rule a second time.

It was Blake who'd get us kicked out, not me.

"Man—" A soft *whump* announced Blake hitting the deck behind me instead of landing on his feet like the wildcat shifter fucking well should have.

Those are some panther display skills right there, my friend. Enough not to get him laid tonight, in any case. But his dry spell wasn't my problem.

"Come on." I strode through the curtain that separated the VIP section from the main club upstairs area, gripping his upper arm. "We aren't coming back until you craft yourself an apology to the club owner and deliver it in person, preferably on your knees with a suitable sense of grovel, am I fucking clear?" I seethed.

"Yes, Gray. It's clear," Blake mumbled.

I towed him out the back door and into the alley behind the club the staff used for smoke breaks. Shattered glass skittered around my boots as I gave him a hard stare. "Clear?"

"Yes!" He threw his hands up. "Fucking clear, all right? I'm sorry I let her get to me. She smelled like a bitch in fucking heat and all I could think about was sinking into her. Like she called to me or something." He rubbed the back of his neck where I grabbed him on the stage.

A twinge of guilt hit me for handling him so roughly. *Only in bed for that shit.* Getting run out of Canada still shit me. I'd make it up to him later. But this couldn't be a lesson soon forgotten.

"Better be," I barked, letting his arm go to rake my fingers through my hair. I got that he felt bad. I did too, but that didn't change anything. "Twice, Blake. Twice you've done this. First home, now here—"

A tiny sound turned both our heads, halting me mid-tirade. A sound like a wounded animal.

I frowned, sourcing the noise that could have come from a child, but didn't. Her scent hit me first, a wave of sweet and salty and full of desperate, unchecked *need.*

Freedom, clear skies, and new moons.

The darkest of nights. Feralness and hidden secrets under a moon I had no name for. That's what I inhaled. The nights when I could shift and run for fucking hours. Kill and feast and wear the blood of whatever got in my way. Fuck, too, if that's what hit me. And right now...

Blood rushed through my body, her scent calling my beast to the surface. I shucked off my jacket before I could think the action through, too caught up in the moment as her need wrapped around me. Hell, I hadn't seen her yet, didn't know where she was, but I was ready for her.

Shadows rippled under my skin. My vision darkened, narrowing to a pinpoint. A single glance at Blake showed me he was on the cusp of his own shift, fighting for control too.

I swung about, searching for the source.

In the far corner of the alley, amongst the rubbish and discarded trash curled a filthy creature, all skin and bones and matted hair. Lips parted to display white teeth as she gasped and cried. But I could barely focus on whatever hurt her.

If need has a scent, this girl is it.

She was ours, and we both knew it. This was our mate. We'd never bothered to try to find someone who suited us both, not after the debacle at college, and that had been over ten years ago. But what this girl had … whatever ran through her blood was undeniable. *Undeniably ours.*

Three fast strides as the alley walls blurred, the nightclub's pounding tempo muted behind double brick, I crouched at her side and cupped her face.

Her scent was stronger here, and it took everything in me not to ruin my last goddam suit.

"Who are you? Can you tell me your name?" I rasped, my throat thick with the desire to hold her, lick her skin clean. Mark her as ours.

Thick lashes fluttered over closed eyes that ever so steadily rose to meet mine. My world stopped. Somewhere behind me, Blake swore.

Her eyes were ringed in a galaxy of purple

starlight.

VOLUME FOUR

Chapter Two

Lottie

I could barely see the man crouched before me through the violet haze that obliterated everything in the world, turning it all into fields of black and purple. Even the person in front of me resembled a twisted nightmare, though I learned not to trust my senses days ago.

"Looks like bait."

The words didn't make sense to me as I returned to my ruminations. How long had I been in this place? Not that long. A week? I had no idea. Focus was impossible. Every time I tried to stand my stomach wanted to revolt. Gravity meant nothing when my field of vision resembled a swirling galaxy painted on the inside of my eyeballs.

"Sweetness." A different voice attacked me from the side.

I turned my blurred eyes toward this new form, finding a gaze of pale green that filtered through my haze like he could see me in the mess my head had become. Without my permission my hands raised to touch, and the man stilled. I encountered bristles, a defined jaw, a warm face.

He laughed softly. "Yeah, that's me. You gonna let us take you somewhere so you can clean up? Eat, maybe put something on?" He kept his voice light, but I recognized the strain beneath it, what he wasn't saying.

You're a mess. I don't know if you're a victim or the threat, but I need to find out.

The silence on the other side of me didn't say anything else, though a hard, calloused hand found mine and gripped hard. I anchored to a firm grip, knowing instinctively this unyielding man wouldn't let me fall, and the warm face I clutched, though I couldn't see either of theirs, and nodded.

The world jerked with me.

"All right," I managed, before I retched bile and stomach acid on the alley floor because that was all I had left in my body to vomit.

****

Warmth covered me in a deep sense of safety and protection. I snuggled in, resting my cheek against the hard/soft surface that beat a pleasant, steady thump beneath me. Something stroked along my spine in an idle rhythm, neither lazy nor slow, but *safe*. I let out a contented sigh.

"If you keep doing that, we might not give you back."

Happy bubble popped.

"We?" I sat up too fast, and the room rocked.

White sheets, dark gray flooring, and heavy wooden exposed beams were all I saw before I covered my mouth with my hand, hoping to prevent a repeat of my last movement. Then my stomach settled along with the room, the ability to see registered, and all-encompassing warmth hit me on both sides, at least from the waist down.

A chill cooled my skin where the covers dropped from my bare flesh. I stared side to side, squishing first in one direction as I came face to nipple with an enormous pec—the one I slept on—and above that, unyielding gray eyes. Black hair hung over a carved face in longer strands, and an evening shadow coated his chin.

This is the first man who spoke to me.

Even with my addled mind I knew that. But the

way he watched me, cold and fiery all at once, left me scrambling for breathing room, my prior nausea forgotten.

When my scrambling butt hit something warm on that other side, I twisted and rediscovered the owner of the green eyes. Much easier to look at in all the ways. His mouth curved in a grin he covered with his hand a second too late. Tanned skin covered him in a never-ending expanse decorated with ridges of muscle. High cheekbones and a playful gleam in those moss green eyes leant him a less terrifying edge than the first man.

It wasn't until I stilled, staring at him, that an arm snaked around my waist to hold me to the hard chest of the unyielding black-haired man with the gray eyes who scared the shit out of me. I lay between the two men who saved me and realized that not one of us wore a single stitch of clothing. And that for the first time in days— weeks—*months*—I was clean. Someone had showered me. I smelled like … flowers. Just flowery soap. And maybe a strange sharp male tang.

Everything was so right it was all wrong.

"I shouldn't be here," I breathed, not actually sure where *here* was.

"You're right where you should be, love." Green Eyes caught a lock of my hair and twirled it around his fingers, lulling me closer to him inch by inch as his smile grew wider. "You shouldn't be anywhere but with us ever again."

I shivered at the underlying promise in his words, barely able to recall my own name as he tugged me closer. His breath brushed my lips before a growl and a sharp tug broke us apart.

"Stop it." The arm around my waist tightened as harsh words were directed over my head to the green-eyed man. A second later I found myself on my back staring into eyes the color of an overcast day. No, not overcast—like a breaking summer storm. "How do you feel?"

"Uh…"

My singular sound was interpreted in different ways by the pair of men who peered down at me. Well, the green-eyed one peered. Gray just stared.

"You're scaring the shit out of her," Green Eyes stage-whispered behind his hand. "Why don't we feed you, love? What do you like to eat?"

"Stop fucking flirting," the black haired, gray-eyed man snapped. "We can feed you in a minute. I need to know if you're all right first." His gaze roamed over my body like he wanted to devour me, though the only place we touched were where his thighs pressed to mine, and—

That's not a thigh.

I gasped and made the hellish mistake of glancing down. Laughter met my ears and I turned tomato red or some other pink hue as my body basically self-combusted on the spot. "I'm fine," I said hurriedly, scrambling backward up the bed but the man with three logs for legs and, um, other things, came with me.

"That's not an answer," he growled.

The sound froze me mid-scramble. "Sorry," I whispered in a voice so small I could barely hear it.

"You scared her," said the other man reprovingly.

"Fine," growled my gray-eyed giant. "Let's start again. What's your name, pet?"

I blinked at him, trying to find it. My memory blanked on me, and I frowned.

"It's easy, okay?" said the green-eyed, tanned man. "I'm Blake. This behemoth is Gray. You knee him any time you want, all right?" he added helpfully.

I smiled for what felt like the first time in an age.

"Cute," I muttered. "I figured you'd be called something like that. I'm L…" My brain froze again.

Gray's eyes narrowed. *At least his name makes sense.* "What did you take last night, pet?" he asked in a softer voice. Smoother.

My body reacted to him like it had to the green-eyed Blake when he tugged on my hair earlier. Prickles rioted along my arms as Gray loomed over me, a deep sound originating in his chest that set every particle in the room on edge.

Every piece of *me* reacted to him.

"Taken? Like—I wasn't drunk, just homeless," I whispered. Memory slammed into me with the confession. "I was homeless. My ex kicked me out, ended my career months ago. Stripped my bank account. His name was the one on the lease and he refused to give me a reference, so no one would look at me." I shrugged. "He was an asshole. Cut me off from friends. Family doesn't want to know me. Toxic, and I get that now. Control freak. I lived on the streets for a few weeks. A month, maybe. Did what I had to survive. So now you know what I am, you can go right ahead and kick me out of your nice warm bed—"

"I'm not kicking you out of anywhere," Gray snapped, bracing his forearms either side of my head while his legs wedged their way between mine, spreading my thighs wide. Warmth on one side told me Blake hadn't moved, though his hand slid along my arm to entangle our fingers.

"Subtle, Gray," he muttered.

"Your name," Gray repeated. "I'm glad the ex is gone. I'm *glad*"—he shot a look at Blake that should have turned him to ash on the spot—"that you're safe. But this would be better if I had your name, pet."

"Why?"

Blake huffed. "Humor him." His fingers squeezed mine.

"Lottie," I whispered, glad my two remaining brain cells functioned for a brief moment. "Just Lottie."

Gray's pupils blew out as he took my name and tried it out on his tongue, Blake whispering reverently along with him. "Lottie," he murmured. "Thank you."

Then he lowered his mouth, grazing the corner of my lips with his, licked along the slope of my neck before I could exhale a startled breath, and bit me. *Hard.*

I screamed before a hand clamped over my mouth. Tears gathered in the corners of my eyes and overflowed as Blake stared down at me, his face not without compassion.

"I'm sorry, sweetness. It's sort of necessary," he murmured.

"Arrroooiteeeooo?" I mumbled around his hand when breath resumed, along with my heartbeat. I winced as Gray retracted his teeth, and warmth heated the area. My hands dug into his shoulder but he didn't seem to care I marked him the way he had me.

Blake stroked my jaw as his fingers relaxed gently when he realized I wasn't going to keep screaming. "I might," he murmured ruefully. "But I'll give you more warning than he did."

Gray groaned into my throat, pushing my thighs further apart as he licked and sucked at the throbbing site of the bite mark. I inhaled sharply, a shuddering breath left me a second later as a rush of heady pleasure spun my world on its axis. I clutched Blake's hand in case I fell off the bed.

"That hurt," I accused Gray, flexing the fingers that dug into his shoulders. He didn't stop his ministrations, just kept going in a rhythm that wasn't comfortable but felt like ... an apology. Each lick soothed the pain, took me into a sleepy, dozy state. "Why did you do that?" I asked, trying not to yawn.

There was something I should be asking. Something so very important that I couldn't let slip my mind right now…

Gray lifted his head, his lips garnet and glossed with my blood. "Because you're my mate," he muttered. "And if I didn't claim you then I could have fucking well killed you."

"That's nice," I murmured as my eyes shut.

I tumbled into a world where the two men fought over my head from a distance and I didn't care anymore. Where my memories floated away, just beyond my ability to grasp them, but then they didn't matter either. All I wanted was to sink and drift and never wake up again.

Even when Blake called my name urgently, his hands cupping my face, moss green eyes staring deep into mine. I tried to reach him too but just like everything else, I couldn't.

And so, I drifted.

VOLUME FOUR

Chapter Three

Blake

I thought we lost her when Gray pulled that stupid fucking stunt and marked her.

"All because you couldn't wait," I groused. Thick shadows roiled beneath my skin, and my beast agreed, ready to tear free of my chest and rip into him.

It had been years since Gray and I fought, *really* fought. He was stronger than me, and faster too, if only by the slightest margin. But in his distracted state, I could take him.

We were both distracted with *her*. She would be the thing that ruined us.

"Has the bleeding stopped?" I paced at the foot of the bed, unwilling to settle beside Lottie for fear of tearing her newly healed wound open.

Gray marked her, so it was also his right to heal her. Panthers usually traveled and mated alone but we were a special package deal. We had never expected to find our *one*, either of us, yet here she was.

"It's stopped." Gray slid a hand behind Lottie's head where I placed a towel so she wasn't lying in the pool of blood that nearly ended her life. "She's all right."

"You don't know that until she's awake." I was as close to ripping out the hair I had left as I'd ever come. "How could you be so stupid? Careless?" I shouted the words, uncaring if our neighbors heard us.

Hell, if—*when*—she got better, they'd all hear worse things than our fighting.

"I didn't hit an artery if that's what you're thinking," he said tersely. "Whatever was in her system acted like an anticoagulant. Blood thinner." He glanced up at me. "Though that's not the correct term, but it will do for these purposes."

I ignored the rest of his explanation. I was out for blood and he was who I needed. "She said she hadn't taken anything."

"Then like with you, she was … assisted."

"No one gave me anything," I objected before the penny dropped. "Wait. You think someone tried to date-rape me?"

"Essentially." Gray stopped fussing long enough to look up at me. "Or someone who wants shifters to come into the open in a very, very bad way. What were you doing when I pulled you off that stripper again?"

I stared at him. "I don't remember. Anything. Where … *fuck*!" I shouted at the ceiling. The neighbors would hate us after this. We'd be lucky not to receive an eviction notice. *Again.*

Gray nodded as though he expected the outcome. "It was the same for her. Did you see Lottie struggle to find her own name? Hers was a massive dose, or maybe on her being a human, it hit harder. I don't know. She has a mark, here." He pushed her hair aside to show a small reddish dot on the back of her neck where her hair would have concealed it and otherwise grit and dirt.

"The hell?" I reached out and pulled back, scared I'd damage her more.

Gray nodded. "That she just happened to be our mate could have turned into something ugly. What if we were shifters without a code? There are plenty of those around. She was naked, outside a nightclub, had no sense of herself…" He shrugged, though the unease that swept through me at his explanation lingered in his eyes.

I knew he hated she'd been in that situation and we hadn't been there to help her, even though we hadn't known her then. That *he* hadn't been there. I knew, because I felt exactly the same way.

"She was bait," I whispered, repeating Gray's words from the alley that hadn't made sense then but clicked over now. My throat clogged with bile. I forced the stomach acid back to it space as I looked down at her. *Hell be damned.*

I climbed onto the bed on her other side, my jeans brushing her legs as I settled beside her, running my fingers along the mark Gray left on her. Purple edged the bruise so deep it was almost black in spots. She'd bear his mark forever, a shadow roiling beneath her skin. A part of his beast slept inside her that would respond to him in a way no one else ever would. She'd understand him like no one else ever could. Including me.

My heart ached. "I want that," I whispered, tears pricking my eyes. I blinked them away as he lifted her still form in his arms and passed her to me. I took her with a reverence I never knew I possessed.

"She's ours, Blake. Mark her. Feel her soul melding with yours." He rubbed his own neck and I knew the damage he did to her revisited on him ten times over, only the mark she left on him would remain invisible.

"No," I snapped, cradling her close. "I'll mark her when she asks me, and not a moment before."

Gray met my eyes. "And if she never asks?"

Panic gripped my stomach, and I bent over like I'd been stabbed, still clutching her to my chest. "Then I'll live without it," I answered him, the lie bitter on the back of my tongue like acid still resided there.

Gray offered me a smile I hated.

"No," he said softly. "You won't."

****

I made our girl coffee and hoped she preferred that over tea, or else I needed to go shopping in a hurry. Her story ripped me up from the inside out. The dick who threw her out—who she left—deserved death. Flaying. I made up fresh tortures as I collected food for her on a tray. I had no idea what else she liked so I made her a bit of everything. Tiny sandwiches with the crusts cut off, a bowl of fruit salad, nuts rubbed in curry powder, even miniature quiches I cooked myself in the oven I knew Gray had never used.

He watched me potter with the final results of my labors from his place standing sentinel at the end of the bed like he had for the past hour, while she began to stir, drinking his whiskey and saying nothing. Guilt hit him hard. He hadn't meant to hurt her, but he fucked up anyway. Pride sucked especially when he put himself on the tallest pedestal in the room.

Me? I was used to fucking up. I'd been doing it all my life. Figured I still had a fair few rounds to go, too. But that didn't mean I would stop trying to get it right in between times. Like now, with Lottie.

I slid the bamboo tray over her lap as she stirred on the pillow pyramid I made for her, trying to elevate her so she wouldn't accidentally open the wound and bleed out on us when we weren't looking. Never had I realized how fucking fragile humans were until one became my mate.

I didn't know the first thing about humans except that they ate a lot of crap, stayed inside their houses instead of enjoying the wilds, and collected shit they didn't need. Shifters tended to be a more outdoorsy bunch on the whole. Our lifestyle ranged toward the more minimalistic end of the extreme. How Lottie would fit into that, I wasn't sure.

She'd been on the streets for a bit. That much was

clear. Her body sank into the puffy bed that wasn't ours to start with like someone wiped all the stress from the tight lines of her too-thin body. Every muscle and tendon in me strained at the thought that my mate wasn't looked after. I needed to care for her, make sure she was all right.

But also ... I couldn't let her go. Even if she begged with that pretty mouth. Not just yet.

From the look in Gray's eyes that matched his name and his mood to perfection, he understood that need just fine. Still, he pushed back onto his haunches kneeling beside the bed, though his eyes never left her. His fingertips either. Those trailed along her slim form where I tucked her possessively into my arms and glared at him. The first for marking her without her permission, the latter for leaving her.

"I need to speak to them. Explain this," he said softly. Even his beast, usually so close to the surface, sank back deep inside him, quiet with her around.

She's ours.

I know.

I held his gaze as we communicated with glances alone. It had been the same with us since our fathers left us alone on a camping trip when we were kids and never came back. And when we went home...

Shaking myself out of the memory, I offered Gray a sharp nod. "I've got her. Don't be long." *Or I might steal her away.* I didn't say that last, didn't dare voice the desire that lay so deep within me and yet so close to the surface. I knew we shared her, that she called to both of us. Truth be told, she'd be safer between both of us than she ever would be with either of us alone. Our history proved that.

"I'll be back soon. Don't go anywhere." Gray's gaze lingered on her when his touch dropped away. "We need answers."

"So will she."

His mouth tightened, but he didn't answer me as he shifted, the force of the change throwing his face into a monstrous twist I could have interpreted as aggression had I been anyone else but his best friend, and the shifter who shared his mate. His lover.

Had I been anyone else.

Damn good thing I wasn't. I didn't watch Gray leave, already lost in stroking Lottie's soft hair back from her face over the slope of her marred skin. Even though it wasn't my mark and my saliva would do little to ease the ache, I licked her wound anyway, enjoying the way her breathing settled and how she moaned a little in her sleep.

Hell, with only the two of us in the room, I could pretend it was my name she whispered as I breathed in her scent and wished it was my mark she wore. Because I sure as fuck wouldn't place mine on her until she begged me.

And she will beg.

Chapter Four

Gray

I strode through what felt like enemy territory even though it wasn't, my senses attuned to every shifter who thought they hid in the shadows. They failed. New York City wasn't anywhere near our natural habitat, and panthers–pumas, jaguars—I never did give a fuck about wildcat labels—were never created with packs in mind. Or high density living in cities.

This alley that led to a small rabbit warren of a panther community was cloistered between a pair of buildings like a void between reality and the underground. It grew tighter with every step I took into its seething depths.

Seeing so many of my kind in one place when there were less than a hundred rumored in existence across the entire damn planet—due to a lack of exactly what rested in my bed tucked up with Blake—left me uncomfortable to the level of the prickly variety. The things cities do to our kind.

My senses were overloaded, overstimulated already with an excess of sound, lights, and electricity throwing off my judgment. And nothing in this world could convince me that the cement structures were anything more than giant cages keeping humans in. Somewhere along the line, shifters got caught up in the mess of it all, and here we were.

"I didn't think you would come back."

A voice I didn't think I'd hear again called from the depths of the shadows. Lionel Griffin took responsibility for the New York City panther claw. That didn't mean he spoke for all of them, however. Plenty of his group of shifters sidled along the shadows and maintained their distance in a not-so-respectful manner.

I huffed out a short breath, remembering our last conversation that ended in a poorly veiled threat that told me I shouldn't bother crossing their territory again. Apparently, the head of this claw didn't like competition. Not that I had any interest in politics, local or otherwise.

"Neither did I." I slid my hands into my pockets and the masses crept an inch forward. A smile that bared my teeth crossed my face. "What do you know about a drug that brings on heat?"

"Heat?" He made several strange clicking sounds with his tongue and the creeping claws backed the fuck up in a hurry, though plenty mistimed their exit. That maneuver needs practice. Way too loud for my taste. Not that I'd be here long enough to care about his sloppy defensive tactics. "Are you trying to get pregnant, Alpha?" That last came out with a solid dose of sarcasm. "I can arrange for you to be fucked up, if that's your goal."

A different shadow crossed the alley's threshold at the far end, less lithe than the usual panther shifter. Almost double my height, this shifter had to be half damn bear or some other cross variety.

"King Kong can step down for the night," I murmured, knowing my voice would travel as my father had taught me, and nearly winced at the recollection, still painful at the loss after all these years. For myself and Blake both. *Nearly.* But I knew better than to show weakness in front of strange shifters. "My brother was date-drugged. I want to know the source."

"Why?" Lionel stepped up beside his champion.

I let my eyebrows rise. "Why? So I can beat the shit out of them. Come on, Griffin. Tell me you wouldn't do the same to your little brother's abuser." I tipped my head to one side, meeting the panther's eyes.

He watched me, humor slipping off his face at the mention of his invalid brother. A shameful mention, in his eyes, though I didn't give a shit. The boy needed protection, not his brother's disgust at his condition.

"Was Blake date-raped?" He laughed at the thought.

Hell, I would join him, thinking of the stripper humping away at him on the stage floor as the shift tried to force its presence due to whatever got injected into him. The same as Lottie, only she had nothing to shift into. Only drive us mad.

Bait.

Christ, it could have been so much worse if it hadn't been us. If it had been anyone else. Shifter or human, she'd been left vulnerable in every way. I regretted my haste in marking her, but at least now she was ours. Mine, for now. Blake would mark her in time and then his claim on our mate would be uncontestable, as it should be.

"Cute. So, you know nothing about the person baiting shifters in your territory, Alpha?" I threw his term back at him, terms panthers hadn't used in a generation, back when half of us had been wiped from the planet. "Leaves them with purple eyes."

When Blake and I both lost our parents in a single night, and woke up orphans on a teen's camping trip. The day we started to run together and never stopped.

That we also discovered our mate together sat well with me, strengthened our bond. If Blake could just get his stubborn head past that first part, he'd be able to see the same future I did for us all: the three of us heading to a state we'd never been to, slinking into the wilderness. Disappearing and forming a family there. We needed no one except the three of us.

Even as I formed the thought in full, I knew it as a pipe dream.

Fuck, I was as bad as Blake. Worse, maybe. Craving what we never had as kids.

"Are you accusing me of not having control of my territory?" Lionel roared loud enough to shake the buildings either side of us to their foundations.

I didn't move, just watched him, and nodded. Once.

"Something like that."

Lionel didn't move. His champion remained still. The alley fell into complete and utter silence. After a power move like that, he'd have to be careful the humans didn't call their police and force them out into the streets. Then what would their precious claw do for cover?

No, Blake, Lottie, and I would be much safer traveling small. We couldn't stay here, and from the closed look on Lionel's face, I just wore our welcome right out.

Finally, he shifted, the shadows beneath his skin rippling until he prowled toward me on all fours. Only when he reached me, circling once, then stopping right in front of me, his black fur rippling again to leave him in human form, did he speak.

"You are strong and brave. But can you protect your wayward friend?" Lionel narrowed his eyes at me. Assessing.

"Can you let go of your hatred for your father in order to protect your brother?" I threw back at him, unafraid.

If I died here tonight, Blake would look after Lottie. My regret was that she hadn't been fully herself off the damn drug enough to see me clearly. The edges of her eyes ... those were shrouded in that damn purple. It would be too long if I never saw eyes like that ever again.

"You walk a fine line, Alpha," Lionel smirked. "Don't you care if tomorrow dawns without you?" He nodded to his champion who stalked toward me, a knife glinting dully in his fist.

I shrugged. "I don't care about your politics. We're heading off soon. I just want to know if there are side effects to the damn drug, if she'll be hurting tomorrow."

"*She*?" Lionel's smile widened impossibly.

Fuck.

Keeping my face impassive, I let my eyes half hood. "I assume you know nothing, then." I turned my back on him and started my walk back along the alley. Which seemed a damn long way at this point. Too far. Hell, I'd never make it without finding a blade lodged in my back.

"Alpha," Lionel sneered.

I stopped. Didn't turn.

"I hear good things about that drug. Mate within the first seventy-two hours, and pregnancy is guaranteed."

My heart leaped in my chest. *Breeding.* Fuck me, of course that was the goal. I swallowed the knowledge, keen to move my Northern ass out of the alley. The city. This motherfucking state.

"Then I have an interesting night ahead of me." The throwaway line seemed to appease Lionel.

I made it to the end of the alley without further interruption and headed back toward our apartment, taking several detours. I might not know the source of the drugs, but now I knew its purpose. And Lionel knew plenty. I could circle back to him later.

Right now, I had another goal in mind.

VOLUME FOUR

Chapter Five

Lottie

The borrowed sweatshirt I wore that slipped off my shoulder, because it was five sizes too big for me, smelled of mint and soap. It hung mid-thigh, which was a good thing because there wasn't anything under it. And that scent just matched the green eyes that followed me as I padded around the giant kitchen, clutching my mug of black coffee that scaled my throat with bitter ambrosia syrup.

It was perfect.

So was he.

"Blake," I tried his name out on my tongue. "And Gray." The absent brother? Friend? I made up my mind to ask about that later. Not now. "The one who bit me."

Blake winced. "Yeah. That would be him. I'm sorry about that."

My hand drifted to the tender spot where the dark giant of a man who had lain between my thighs, his weight braced over me, had sucked on my flesh then sank his teeth into me. Then he had licked that same spot until I lost myself in pure pleasure.

Almost as much pleasure as my first hot drink in weeks. I sipped the scalding liquid taking a perverse amount of delight in the pain that slithered along my throat at the overheated liquid that made its way to my belly. *I will never ever have enough of that feeling.* Either of them. The heat, or his … heat.

Blake watched me through wary eyes though they weren't without heat of their own.

"Are you going to bite me too?" I asked

conversationally.

He winced again. "I'm so sorry." He reached for me, then drew his hand back like I was the scalding liquid he couldn't stand.

For some reason, that thought panged in my chest. I placed the mug on the counter, and rounded the corner where he stood with the wide stone-topped bench between us, removing the barrier. He backed up in a hurry.

I stopped, folding my arms. "I'm sorry. I know a street kid in your house is pretty disgusting." I mirrored him, retreating a step. Maybe I'd read him wrong.

Blake shook his head, though he didn't move. "That's not it, Lottie. You're anything but disgusting. I … you're hurt enough. What Gray did … I'm so sorry."

I reached up to touch the mark in the crook of my neck, running my fingers over the tender patch. "I don't understand any of this. I don't understand why I was so…" I waved my hand in front of my eyes to explain the purple haze of before, lost for words.

Blake nodded. "Yeah, me too. I don't know what it was. Gray thinks we were drugged. For, I don't know. I'm sorry you were hurt." He took a slow step forward, reaching out. His fingers grazed my skin where the sweater slipped off my shoulder. "He should have asked," he whispered, reverently.

"I don't understand anything," I repeated, staring up at him.

His fingers rested on the mark, his breaths coming short. "It's a mating mark."

"A *what*?"

"A mating mark. You're our mate." Blake licked his lips.

"He said that before," I recalled. "So, you are going to bite me after all." I backed into the bench where it butted against my spine.

"If you ask me to," he breathed. "But not until then." His pupils dilated, Blake dropped his hands. Skimming them over my arms, along my rib cage, he grabbed my waist. "Everything else, however…"

Blake paused for half a second, the only warning he gave me, before he lifted me onto the benchtop and stepped between my thighs. A gasp left me at the intimate contact. The sweatshirt pushed up to my thighs. I became all too conscious of the fact I wore nothing beneath the material—*his* borrowed clothing. And how tall he stood. Even seated on the bench that pressed halfway up my back when I was at ground level, Blake still stood a full head over me.

"You're a giant," I mumbled, tipping my head back to stare up at him.

"Nah, you're just tiny. I kinda like it," he rumbled, pushing the sweatshirt further up my thighs. "But I'm regretting giving you this. I liked curling around you. Liked feeling you closer." He scooted my butt to the edge of the benchtop, taking the opportunity to slip his hands beneath the material and up to my ribs.

"Blake," I whispered.

"Want me to bite you or kiss you?" he murmured seductively, his lips turning up in a flirtatious smile that made it hard to take him seriously at all, though I knew he meant it.

Both.

"Kiss me?" I whispered back, afraid of what the other meant, and not understanding his rules.

Disappointment flared in his eyes, but he didn't say a word. Rough thumbs played a slow rhythm gliding up and down my waist as he dipped his head. His breath brushed across my lips as I leaned into him, finding the hem of his tee and tugging on it as my eyelids drifted shut.

"Having fun?" Gray cut in. Heavy footfalls I just *knew* he made louder on purpose announced him belatedly.

I ducked my head, hiding in Blake's tee. His arms folded around me in a protective embrace I didn't instantly hate. Resting my head on his chest I listened to them talk then fight, the conflict becoming vague to me as always. Blake's warmth surrounded me. Part of me wished I'd taken up his offer to bite me. Then I realized how insane that sounded, and wanted to slap myself stupid for the mere thought. I didn't survive several weeks on the streets by letting every Gray and his brother bite me whenever they wanted. On cue, my shoulder twinged, and I flinched.

"Are you all right?" Blake pushed my hair back where it fell across my face.

"Is she hurting?" Gray barged in, yanking me from my safe warmth with hard hands and an unyielding face. Cold eyes the color of a storm over the sea studied me.

"She is fine, thank you," I muttered, shoving at his chest. Not that it made any difference whatsoever. "*She* would like some courtesy and warning before *he* barges in from now on. Please," I added, rolling my shoulder.

Gray, predictably, ignored me. "Does it hurt?" He tugged me forward, his grip softening as he cradled me against his larger form. Hot breath brushed my shoulder and before I could question his motives, he was licking my wound again.

"Stop that." I wriggled in his hold but that had the same effect as pushing at him before—*nada*. "You can't be serious," I protested. "Licking is not an apology, unless you're between a girl's legs."

That last fell out, and I had no idea where from. Gray's blustering nature brought out the sass in me.

"Is that so?" He raised his head, locking eyes with me. His gaze shifted, focusing above my head for a second. Then I was airborne and slung across the kitchen bench. Hands crossed behind my head. I whimpered, grasping about as Blake's face came into view.

"Breathe," he murmured, apologetically. "I think you asked for something and Gray is about to give it to you."

A pair of hands pushed my legs open as my bare butt hit the benchtop for the second time. I barely had a second to process that thought before a hot, wet tongue lapped along my pussy.

I cried out, and found Blake's fingers sliding into my mouth, muffling the sound.

"Shhh, Lottie. Let him say sorry in the way he knows best. Just … try not to scream, okay?" His face filled with sympathy as he cradled my head gently, stroking my hair and slid his fingers in and out of my mouth.

I would have thought he wasn't interested in the fact his friend had his tongue inside my cunt except for the hardness pressing to the top of my head that told the lie of his own arousal he denied time and again.

Instead of trying to call him out as he gagged me gently and Gray's tongue drove me slowly wild, I leaned into Blake's embrace, rubbing against his erection. Hearing his soft breaths turn into short, hitched blasts, and watching his eyes dilate as I sucked on his fingers relentlessly as Gray took hold of my orgasm and coaxed it closer became my new favorite pastime.

Blake stared down at me, lips parted as I ached for his friend on the benchtop. My juices covered my thighs as I cried out, my voice muffled by Blake's fingers in my throat. He pumped them relentlessly, his breath panting as fast as mine as Gray licked me faster. He found my clit and swirled the tiny hard nub with his tongue. I closed my eyes, hooking my legs behind his neck, and drew him closer.

Gray gripped my ass in both hands, and pushed a finger inside me. I came fast and hard, the extra sensation throwing me over the edge. My scream was cut off by Blake's fingers in my mouth. I kissed and sucked on them, forcing my eyelids open to watch him.

He groaned above me, still stroking my hair as I rode my orgasm out on Gray's tongue.

"Blake…" I mumbled around his fingers

He bent down. "Say it, Lottie."

"Kiss me?" I looked at him through my lashes.

Breathing hard Blake let me go, stumbling back.

I reached for him, but he kept retreating until he hit the opposite wall. Then my body slid across the countertop and I couldn't see him anymore at all. The next pair of eyes that met mine were gray, and they were anything but cold.

"That was cruel, mate of mine," he reproved me, the undercurrent of his voice a dark ripple that reverberated through me at a soul-deep level.

He'd connected us, and my spirit acknowledged him. What could I do to refuse that?

I swallowed hard and met his eyes. "Should I apologize?"

Chapter Six

Blake

She stole my breath, my heart, and my soul in three tiny words. Hell, I was halfway out the door when Gray stopped my retreat.

"No," he murmured, his gaze still locked on her. His fingers twitched at his side, two straight, the others curled—a signal we made up a decade before out of necessity when we were hunted. When we ran the first time.

Gray's eyes raised to find mine, the corners of his mouth twitching. My cock thickened in response to the way those lips moved, knowing exactly how they felt wrapped around me, making me come when I'd told him to fuck off after a fight and he pinned me down and did me anyway. When he held me afterward and petted me like he did her now.

He's going to fuck her in front of me and there's not a damn thing I can do about it.

I couldn't leave. Nothing would drag me away from the live porn show about to play out for my front-row seat. And I refused to join in until she begged for my bite. My mark.

Taking from her like he had wasn't my style.

This would be a different sort of torture, and Gray knew as well as I did that I was here for all of it.

His hand wound through her clean hair, hair I spent the better part of the evening stroking for the floral notes that elicited from the fine strands, and pulled her head back sharply, exposing her pulse point. His mouth found that, then his mark as he sucked on her soft skin until she moaned beneath him, already half gone. His other hand disappeared between her legs, though I had no doubt he played her body like an instrument designed for him.

Hell, she had been designed for us at a cosmic level. I hadn't believed the fated mates bullshit until I scented her, but here she was. Playboy me would have fucked anything with a glistening pussy and a willing mouth. But now...

Now I'd never leave her side.

Her head dropped back when he released her. Luminous eyes, blessedly free of that freakish purple glow, found mine. Lottie slid her hands over her head, reaching for me with beckoning fingers. Shaking my head though I never tore my eyes away from her—them—I slunk back through the doorway, my claws carving deep arcs in the plasterboard. We'd have to pay for the damage but Gray could cover it. I didn't give a fuck. If this was how he wanted to play, then he could wear the consequences of his screwy life choices.

"Please, Blake?" she begged.

Soft lips parted on my name, but they weren't the words I needed from her.

"Beg for his mark, mate," Gray purred over her, extending his teeth to rake them over my sweater, shredding the fabric to her waist. He plucked one bare nipple into his mouth, sucking hard until she arched off the kitchen bench, her eyes glazed with need. The nipple popped free, the peaked dusky pink bud glistening with his saliva. "Ask for his bite."

My cock surged painfully in my sweats, but I didn't touch myself. Hell, it'd be over in a second if I did, but I'd hold back. Gray knew I'd edge myself to insanity for him ... and now for her, too. And he'd play on that weakness of mine, asshole that he was.

"*Please*." The shaky whisper that left me didn't even sound like my own fucking voice. I clamped my mouth shut, turning away half in disgust at myself but not before the vision of her eyes cleared with a different emotion stopped me cold.

Fear.

This is what Gray did to her, taking from her without asking. I swallowed my own need as he pushed her thighs wide, mounting her there on the kitchen bench, and impaled her on his thick, spined cock.

Her scream he didn't quite catch with his mouth in time was pure bliss. My sweats stained with leaked pre-cum, the material sticking to the tip of my cock as I watched him fuck her. Drawn in, unable to break away as I stood there, the eternal voyeur in a fuck-fest that should have included me.

But I couldn't. I wasn't him.

Gray snarled the moment his mouth unlatched from hers like he heard my thoughts, hated them. He thrust into her with powerful strokes, his knees spreading hers wide as he fucked into her, both of them completely up on the benchtop, their feet hanging off the edge. I didn't care if the damn thing crumbled under their combined weight as long as they didn't *stop*.

She keened beneath him, tiny cries leaving her lips as he sawed into her flesh. I didn't need my shifter senses to know she loved every fucking minute of it. I also knew the moment she came, it would end me. I didn't need my hands working my cock to know that.

Gray's eyes found mine as he licked his lips, smiling demonically as he worked her over. One hand rubbed her arm, sliding up to circle her throat gently. I groaned, my back bowing against the wall, aching for his hands on me in the same way, knowing exactly how that felt—how she felt beneath his power—though she didn't fight him the way I did.

Let him in, let him dominate her. Surrendered in a way I never allowed. I wondered if she would ever do the same for me.

His hand caught beneath her chin, forcing her head all the way back so she stared at me upside down. Those pretty eyes barely found mine, rolling back in her head as her orgasm approached and with it, came mine. My balls tingled, my spine stiffening as my hips jutted out. I needed his hand in my hair, holding me in place while he worked my cock with his fist, forcing me to come for him, spitting into my mouth.

"Watch him come for you. He wants you so badly but denies himself. So come for us both. But. *Watch. Him. Ruin.*"

Her eyes flew open, connecting with me as I shouted my pain and pleasure, the orgasm receding almost as fast as I came on. Cum jetted from my cock to stain my sweats, running down the insides of my thighs as I creamed myself for them in utter, beautiful humiliating disgrace.

"I'll make you lick it up next time," Gray growled at me. He held my gaze a moment longer, softening, almost lovingly before he dragged his attention back to our panting mate. "Now, it's your turn." He slammed into her, and I knew what would come.

The spines his thick cock was covered in at the root thickened, expanding, scraping her walls with every thrust to bring on ovulation. Pain and pleasure mixed, heightening until she was a screaming, cream-lathered mess beneath him. His cum filled her to the brim, overflowing as it soothed the hurts that would remain tender for hours, reminding our mate who owned her.

The way he stayed inside her, still hard for the next minutes, stretching her tender body because he needed to feel her tortured walls pulse around him, worshipping his cock with every weak flutter. Fuck, it was enough to make me hard again, bring out my own spines.

I knew how that felt because that used to be me. Now all I wanted was to slide into her with him, fill her holes and make her body feel used up, sated, warmed and loved by us both.

And all she had to do was ask.

Until then, I slumped against the wall I had destroyed with my claws, and when Gray nodded, I blew them both a kiss, imagining sucking his cock with her for a moment and sharing a three-way kiss. Knowing I'd shower and jerk off to the fantasy for another ruined orgasm because I wouldn't allow myself pleasure until I sank into her or he worked me over, I gave my damp cock and trashed sweats a squeeze as Lottie watched, lust-drunk yet wide-eyed, and walked away.

If I stayed any longer, I might have broken my promise not to touch her until she begged for what I needed.

VOLUME FOUR

Chapter Seven

Gray

Watching Blake walk away shattered me as much as having Lottie in my arms healed me. But half a heart wasn't enough when she needed us both.

"Where's he going?" she murmured, wincing.

I withdrew as gently as I could, knowing she'd be tender as fuck after the way I brutalized her, marking my claim on her body, marking her again as mine.

As long as she lived, my scent would permeate her pores, cling to the walls of her gushing pussy. If Blake got his act together then his scent would mingle with mine, cementing our claim on our mate.

"Because he cares for you," I muttered, running my hands over her body. "Did I hurt you? Much?" I clarified.

"A little." Her impish smile told me everything I needed to know.

She'd be fine, even if I needed to take it easy with her for the next few days. The first mating was always the hardest, and I hadn't been sweet with her. I waited for the familiar twinge of regret but it didn't come this time. Somehow, she knew what to expect of me and accepted that. Accepted me as I came, broken and fucked up and brutal as I was.

"You won't always feel like this." I nuzzled into her neck, inhaling her scent. Committing her to memory.

Lottie was everything my beast and I wanted. I'd have to shift in front of her soon, show her my other more monstrous parts, but first we had a little history to get through. And maybe a future. Because I sure as fuck wasn't going anywhere without her.

"But Blake..." She twisted in my arms as I scooped her up and carried her toward the bedroom.

My thighs ached not with the strain of carrying her but from how I'd knelt over her on the bench. The stonework hadn't done my bones any favors, that was for damn sure.

"Leave him for now, mate." I kissed the top of her head. "He'll come around." *Better be fucking soon, because otherwise he'll feel it.*

"Mhmm." She made a dissatisfied noise in her throat I hated the moment I heard it.

"Fuck it," I muttered, tossing her onto the bed and climbing over her.

"Whoa." Lottie stared up at me with wide eyes. "You're huge all over. I didn't..." She swallowed, her hands and gaze coasting over me.

"Look your fill." I waited patiently while she explored. When I didn't stop her, she scooted lower, running her fine-boned hands across my stomach, then cupping my cock that responded instantly to her touch, hardening on command. "Damn, girl. I'll go again but I don't want to ruin you."

"You won't."

I twisted to look over my shoulder. Blake stood in my doorway, watching us with an amused look on his drawn face. He was already feeling the bond's pull, that much was obvious from his drained color. The lack of energy where he propped himself up covered the unusual lack of hyperactivity he'd always had in excess with a smirk that sent blood roaring to my cock.

"Are you joining us?" I asked pointedly, raising an eyebrow.

You're weak as fuck and it'll get worse every hour you're not with her.

He stared right back at me, his righteousness blaring out—an unusual expression on the shifter-whore of the year who screwed everything in sight that offered it up on a platter regardless of gender. What a hill to die on, quite literally.

Not that I thought he would die, but his stubbornness issues were a real damn problem. We weren't on home soil. We rented an apartment in the middle of a city we both hated with no plan of what came next with a brand-new mate and a panther claw who despised us.

And a drug habit that hit two of the people I cared about most in the world.

"Join us," I murmured, softening my tone. "She needs you, Blake." *We need you.*

He nodded. "I'll join you. But no mark until you ask for it, sweetness. Whenever you're ready." He sauntered into the bedroom, trailing his fingertips along the back of my thigh displaying all the energy and playfulness he always had.

I knew what that cost him—the show he put on—and hated the fact my cock surged in Lottie's hand.

She glanced between us with wide eyes. "Are you two together?" she asked in a hushed voice.

I shrugged. "He lets me dominate him sometimes," I said easily. Not a lie, but an asshole move. Blake would hate it and he'd hate what I'd do when he put the brakes on the moment he acted out.

His fingertips traced along the base of my spine as he reached between my legs to caress my balls while Lottie worked my cock. "He likes to think he's in control. But you can top from the bottom, sweetness. It's not a … hard … ask." He stroked my balls until I groaned.

The sound reverberated around the room as I took their ministrations, barely grasping that last straw as they gently manipulated me. For as rough and brutal as I could be in bed, this gentle handling, their worship, undid me.

I caught Lottie's wrist in a firm, if sweet, grip and eased her hand back, giving myself some breathing room. Holding her eye, I waited until she nodded and then I reached back and gripped the top of Blake's head by his hair, wrenching him between us all.

"The fuck you think you're doing, playing with me?" I snarled when he stumbled, lacking the strength or energy or pretty much anything at all to resist me. "Did I say I allowed that? Fuck, I nearly came all over our mate. If I had, you'd be cleaning us both up. Actually…"

Mashing our mouths together, I pushed my tongue between his lips. Blake opened for me, sucking on my tongue eagerly though he lacked his usual fervor that would have had us wrestling with all our strength for dominance across the bed. Normally fists would have flown until I pinned him down and worked him over until we were both spent in a puddle of cum and sweat, his hole gaping while I teased him some more.

His moans increased and when I pulled back, I found Lottie stroking her hands all over his back and stomach, exploring him. My smirk matched her coy little smile.

"You said we're all mates, right? That means all of us, not just you and me, and me and him, right?"

I nearly dropped Blake's head, tightening my grip on the asshole just in time to find his startled gaze I was sure matched mine in everything but color.

"That's right, sweetness," Blake breathed. "We're all mates together. Forever."

"Then fucking well mark her," I growled.

He shook his head. A small, suicidal smile played on his lips. "No."

I snarled again, having no idea what the hell he

was playing at, but I'd had enough of his bullshit for one night. "Fine." I shoved him forward and down, so he face-planted in my lap. "If you don't want to bite, then you can suck instead."

Fully expecting to find his teeth imprinted on my flesh, I had the pleasant surprise of welcoming his hot mouth around my leaking cockhead. His tongue wrapped around my length, wetting me nicely before he deep-throated like I taught him, making those delicious gagging sounds.

Lottie watched him, pure joy lighting her pretty eyes as she played with his hair. "I want to help," she whispered, glancing shyly up at me.

I swallowed back a wave of arousal that nearly had me shooting a second load straight down Blake's throat. "Come here." I gestured for her to straddle my hips, leaning back to let Blake work.

She straddled me high, her ass bumping his shoulders. "Like this?"

"Yeah." I cupped her chin and drew her mouth to mine, kissing her deeply while our mate sucked me hard. A soft groan left me as she ground against my stomach, and the sounds that came from her were a whole lot more frustrated. "Want more, honey?"

"Yes. I want both of you."

Blake released my cock from his throat, taking time to lave my balls with his tongue before he rolled onto his back and gripped her thighs, pulling her down onto me.

Lottie whimpered, spreading herself wide as her nails dug into my shoulders. "Oh, that's really—"

"Sore?" I added, glancing down at where Blake positioned himself beneath us and made a vee with my raised knees to support her and give him room to work. "Blake's gonna help you with that, honey. Let him soothe you, okay? He's gonna make you feel like a fucking queen."

I knew the moment she bottomed out and he licked around her swollen flesh where my cock stretched her a second time. Her eyes flew wide, and barely a breath later her head tipped back on a long moan, though her nails still dug into my shoulders.

"Good?"

"So good," she murmured, letting us both take her weight in the ultimate trust exercise as she gave herself over.

She might not wear both our marks yet, but she had accepted Blake. He had to fucking know that, or his stubbornness issues had blinded him to a girl who had already fallen in love with his crooked version of fucked-up chivalry.

"We're gonna stay just like this." I gathered her close, letting my cock thicken inside her. My spines filled out in her heavy warmth, nestling into her tender walls. If she moved, I'd scrape her again. That meant both pain— and a deluge of pleasure. A single thrust would bring her to orgasm, again and again. She'd flood us both with her slick. That could come after. Right now, Blake offered himself up as tribute and we would be the lesser mates to ignore him.

Lottie nestled into my shoulder, letting her cheek rest against my neck as I traced patterns on her back, pretending I didn't want to fuck her senseless while Blake licked around her swollen flesh, stroking the base of my cock and my laved balls with his tongue. The sensations rippled along my spine until I was ready to blow my load inside my girl without ever moving. Then, curling one hand around the back of her neck and holding her tight in place, I began to move. Slow at first then faster I pummeled into her, running one wave of pleasure into the next while she shattered in my arms, screaming my name into my shoulder.

And all the while I sawed in and out of our mate, Blake lay beneath us, licking and sucking at my balls, flicking his tongue around the edges of her cunt to soothe the damage I created. His tongue left warm stripes on my tingling sac until I came with a roar, settling myself deep inside her.

Lottie sobbed softly into my chest, overwhelmed with everything we did. And when I pulled out to get her a warm washcloth, my cum dribbling from her tender hole, I settled her over Blake's waiting mouth where he licked and sucked and soothed her until her cries became moans. I returned to find her riding out her last orgasm of the night on his face as the sun rose across the windows in a fragmented display of golden light. She collapsed in my arms, letting both of us clean her, and was out before I could tell her what my heart already knew.

One night with my mate and I loved her. I'd always love her.

Which meant that drugs and the ex were my problem. Something to be fixed before we left New York City. And I had the feeling we wore out our welcome a few nights before.

VOLUME FOUR

Chapter Eight

Lottie

"I want to kill the ex."

"Fuck off. I called dibs."

"You can do the drug runner. If you can find him."

"Sounds like a second-rate deal to me."

My head swung back and forth as I stared between my two instant lovers of last night while they bantered my past for a future between them.

"You can't kill anyone," I blurted, holding up both hands and ignoring the toast Blake made me.

Both of them stopped talking and looked at me after exchanging glances.

Oddly, it was Blake who answered. "Why not?" he asked politely.

I stared. "Because you can't just go around unaliving people. That's not how the world works."

Gray laughed, getting up from the table. One moment I was looking at a tall brooding man who screwed me to within an inch of my life the night before. Then I stared at the blank space he had filled. At waist height I found the giant black wildcat that prowled around my barstool at the breakfast bar in the kitchen where half the shenanigans went down the night before.

My body still thrummed from all the attention and I hurt a bit too, though they both helped that ache leave with their magic saliva. But even cactus cocks weren't able to prevent me from shrinking at the appearance of a giant cat leaping onto the breakfast bar where Gray had stood beside me a moment before.

"You have got to stop doing that," I cussed him. "I believe you, all right? I get it. We're mates. It's magical. You're a giant black pussy. It's fine."

Blake snorted coffee out of his nostrils and across the kitchen, then spluttered the remainder into the sink. "Fuck me, sweetness. I don't think anyone but you would have the balls to call Gray a big black pussy. But you go right ahead and see if you don't wear yourself a spanking shortly."

I raised an eyebrow. "Any spankings will have to wait for another day."

A literal shimmer and black kitty turned into a regular male again. Naked, and ginning in my face, and standing beside me this time. Let's be honest. A grinning Gray seemed weird as all get out. Maybe weirder than the giant black pussy.

"She has spoken." His mouth turned down as he surveyed me. "I want to know more about this ex who threw you out onto the streets."

It was my turn to be uncomfortable. "I don't want to talk about him." *Ever.* "He was just a loser."

That I walked away without Brad following me, stalking me as per his usual M.O. was a minor miracle in itself.

"What about your time in the alley?" he pushed. "How were you given the drug?"

That earned another shrug from me. "I don't know, okay?" That came out terse. I softened my tone, or tried to when Blake swapped a glance with Gray and reached for my hand. I let him have it, enjoying the rough feel of his calluses, the larger, all-encompassing warmth of him.

He might be submissive to Gray, but to me he was everything. I couldn't imagine my life without these two—black cats—whatever the hell they counted as, not now that I had found them.

I didn't know how I would exist if they disappeared as suddenly as they arrived in my life. It was like we were all tethered together. A pull at my chest came with every micro-expression, every intonation I picked up in their unspoken exchanges.

"Sure there wasn't something, sweetness?" Blake's thumb rubbed back and forth across my pulse point at my wrist in a hypnotic rhythm. "A person, someone you agreed to do something for…"

He didn't say "offer services like a whore," but he may as well have.

A deep growl reverberated through Gray's chest as he stalked toward me, the strings winding us together pulling in both directions at once and suddenly it was all too much.

"Stop." I scrambled backward, pulling my hand out of Blake's hold. "I need you to stop and not come any closer," I warned both of them, still retreating across the kitchen. Tiled floor turned to carpet and still my feet kept moving.

Blake watched me carefully, making not a single move, though Gray leaned forward and I knew the moment I ran he'd be on me. And I couldn't outrun him. I wasn't sure I wanted to outrun him.

A knock on the apartment door saved us all.

"Bathroom," I muttered and broke away, trotting quickly to the main room rather than the smaller en suite the boys both used that led off the bedroom.

Right now, I just wanted to have a room to myself, sit on the floor, and panic attack all over the place without their watchful eyes bearing down on me. Perfect they might be, amazing the call to them, but also too much all at once.

I'd known them for a handful of hours. Gray had

fucked me into submission along with Blake several times, and I couldn't take much more of his attention for a while. My insides felt like they had been scraped raw, over-sensitized to the point I was afraid if I jumped up and down on the spot, I'd orgasm right in front of him if he so much as touched me.

And his kisses. Those were the all-encompassing sort. I craved Gray's kisses like they were an addiction. Sliding my back to the bathroom door the moment I was inside, I did not need to turn on the light as the rising sun illuminated every crevasse, removing the need to hide within the shadows. I settled on the cold, unyielding tiles and rested my cheek on my knees. The tee Gray gave me—one of his after he shredded the sweatshirt Blake provided before—rose up leaving me chilled and numbed. The warmth from the boys in the kitchen dissipated with their absence. Because I chose to run from them. But here, for a minute, I could breathe.

"Lottie?" Blake knocked on the bathroom door. "Checking you're okay, sweetness. Nothing more, all right?"

"Can't a girl pee in peace?" I lied.

He chuckled. "'Course you can. But you're also full of shit."

"That obvious, huh?"

"I might not know you, but I *know you*, sweetness. You're ours as much as we are yours."

My chest warmed and tightened all at once, both accepting and rejecting what he said. I craved the connection, panicked at the thought of having no choice.

But I want to stay with them. Never leave.

And that gut reaction scared me more no matter how much I wanted it.

"Yeah, that's not confronting at all to a girl who had nothing less than twelve hours ago," I admitted, biting my lip.

Blake laughed, the door creaking as he leaned his weight against it from the other side. "It's a change," he said softly. "Gray ... he's been my brother in the family, sort of, for so long that when we turned to each other out of need for comfort one night it just seemed right. He tell you what happened to our parents?"

"No." Blood filled my mouth as I bit through my lip and I sucked on the wound, wincing, and was glad he wasn't there to see the self-inflicted damage, knowing he'd sass me for it.

Blake sighed. "Back then, we were hidden. No one was supposed to know about shifters. Some did, of course. It happened. But we had no community except a few small families. Panthers don't travel in packs. The local claw here—that's what we call a group of panther shifters—is huge. Out of necessity, I think. Safety in numbers and all. But it's not natural to us. Gray hates being associated with them, does anything to hide away. He'll do anything to hide *you*."

"Oh." I didn't know what else to say. "Thank you?"

"He's very protective of those he loves." Blake let that slip out like it was the easiest thing in the world.

Maybe for him, it was.

"I'm sure he is for you."

A chuckle met my ears, the sound rich and low and filled with tension. "That includes you by default, sweetness. You're his now too, no matter how much you hide it. He accepted you, claimed you, and so he loves you."

"That easy, huh?" My broken whisper was a child's prayer at best.

"That easy." Blake's simple promise left my cheeks damp. "It's okay to be scared. That story I was telling you? Panthers were hunted almost to extinction. We lost our parents in one night. Ran for the next six years. Settled, until I fucked it up and now we're ... well, we aren't running, exactly. Walking, maybe. Until we found you." He paused for breath. "I'll tell Gray you're fine."

I listened to his footsteps retreating up the hallway and let out another breath. After a few more, they came easier. I didn't struggle quite so much with the panic and it receded too. Finally, after my ass well and truly fell asleep, I pushed up on shaking legs that ached nearly as much as my worn-out pussy, and hauled myself in front of the mirror.

The face that stared back at me didn't resemble any human I recognized. I might have expected my face to be gaunt or skeletal, but the twenty-something girl who stared back with silky locks that curled around her shoulders and glowing cheeks, high cheekbones, albeit a bit on the skinny side, didn't resemble a starved homeless girl at all.

Is this who they see when they share me?

I blinked at myself for a stunned moment. Maybe that panther saliva really was that good. Or maybe it had other properties. I had no idea but maybe I needed to find out more about this new world I'd fallen into.

Rummaging through the case of things on the bench that looked like they belonged to Blake from the colors, blue toothbrush, yellow case, minty green swirl glitter toothpaste—everything Gray owned was, well, gray. I brushed my teeth with the borrowed brush and prayed he wouldn't mind.

Mate, remember?

Biting my lip, I practiced my apology a few times once I washed my face and finger-combed my hair, not that it seemed to make much difference. Then I made it to the door. The shadow on the other side told me Blake was back. A smile grew across my face as I rested my forehead against the door.

"You're not going to leave me alone, are you?" I turned the handle and pulled the door inward, stepping back.

A mistake, as it allowed the person on the other side space to step in with me. A person who, from their pasty skin, short stature and dull eyes, was definitely not either of my mates. How quickly I've fallen into their language.

A scream built in my throat but I barely had time to register the dull gleam before a sting hit the side of my neck and the world hazed over. A pretty purple, and the sting reminded me of the last time this happened. At least, I thought it did. Maybe.

Then that memory, and my reality was gone, replaced by the purple haze that blocked the world out of my body, overheated, and all I craved was Gray. Preferably inside me.

Not that I got the chance for that either as I was towed out of the apartment. My mind screamed there was something I should be doing. *Mate, mate, mate!* Like, call for someone, ask for something—*Help me, save me, don't let them!*

But I couldn't form the thought properly in my hazed-out mind.

I don't want to leave.

The face I didn't recognize turned toward me, but I couldn't focus on him either—on anything, really— once we hit the street level, or somewhere beyond it. None of it mattered. Nothing did.

VOLUME FOUR

Chapter Nine

Blake

The bathroom was empty.

"The fuck did she go?" Gray seethed, shoving his way past me.

"The door wasn't locked," I said. My fingers went numb, then my cheeks. "She's not here."

But I just checked on her. My entire body ached, the pains increasing with the distance from her. Panic built as I surveyed the empty space that only confirmed what my mind already knew. *She's gone.*

But no part of me believed that Lottie had run from us. Sure, we freaked her out a bit. Or she freaked out on us. Either way, that was okay, because I would have sworn when I left her in the bathroom a few minutes before, she was just fine. *Fine, fine, fine.*

"The hell did you say to her?" Gray's hand closed around my throat as he shoved me back against the wall.

I didn't bother to fight him. I needed her back as much as Gray but at least he had their mating mark to tether them together. I had nothing.

Whose fault is that?

"I—nothing."

Gray's fingers tightened, constricting my airway. The last time he did this we were playing. This time, his eyes reflected death. Whose was unclear but I was in his sights for messing with our girl.

"I told her about us. All about us," I croaked, pushing the air out. If I was going to die by his hand right now for my sins, then he needed to hear what I said so he would know how to track the girl I must have scared. "I was trying to show her the depth of your love and protection. I didn't mean for this to scare her…" I choked as my vision wavered, though that was from tears at the thought of hurting Lottie, not fear of Gray's rage.

Distress I hated seeing on the alpha's face turned my stomach into a writhing nest of unwelcome parasites.

"We have to find her," he vowed. "Fucking *now*."

"Please," I gasped as his hand opened. I dropped to my knees, sucking in air as he walked away, already shifting. "God, yes."

Gray's panther form headed for the fire escape as his human bulk shimmered into a lithe black cat, though no domestic moggie ever looked like him. Following his lead, I let my beast roam free. The snarl that twinged my vocal cords too low for my human body to cope with hurt but I didn't care. Pain was a small price to suffer for what I'd done if it pushed Lottie away.

I'll find you, sweetness. I'll bring you back. I'll beg you to stay.

Because if she didn't…

I leapt into the daylight, uncaring that we broke all the rules we set ourselves years before, leaping across levels until we scoured the alleys for her scent.

I'll find you.

****

News fucking flash: we didn't find her.

I padded my street grimed kitty ass back into the apartment eighteen hours later none the wiser of how or where our mate had gone. She hadn't left the building at all but her scent lingered around it, though neither of us could understand why for the first hour. But as time passed it became increasingly clear that both of our original assumptions were wrong.

She hadn't left alone. Someone stole our mate.

Gray was inconsolable. And by that I meant everyone who crossed the panther's path met with a flash of claws and teeth before a naked and furious giant of a man accosted them with his fists.

After eighteen hours of hunting and searching and grieving, he followed me back to the apartment, tail low, paws bleeding like mine. Defeated.

Both of us suffered enough minor cuts during our search that not all of them would heal with the shift. Not fast, at least. We were both running on empty. Me more than him, though we both knew why. And neither of us would be able to find Lottie in our condition.

"Sweetness?" I pushed the front door open, scenting for her the moment I walked into the apartment.

But the scent was faint, this morning's Lottie, no later than that.

"She's not here." Gray crossed the threshold and locked the door behind us, his voice flat.

Anyone else might think he'd given up but I knew him better. The longer she stayed away, the worse he'd be until he killed someone. I liked it better when I was the one we worried about.

"Where do you want to try next?" I asked, afraid of his answer.

Gray ran his knuckles through his hair. "I can only think of a few places," he acknowledged. "We go back to the Gin Room, wait and see if she turns up at her old haunts. Stalk the boyfriend if we can find him, but I don't think that's the asshole we need to find. He's not of this world. Just—"

"An asshole," I supplied.

"Yeah." Gray scratched his claw across his scruff. "Or..."

"The NYC Claw," I finished softly, hating the

option. The reliance.

The group might be able to scent what we couldn't. They might know why someone came into our apartment and took what belonged to us. They might know who would be stupid enough to risk Gray's wrath. He was right not to trust them.

Every instinct agreed with him. Shifters weren't meant for city life, especially not our kind. I ached to swim in cold water, submerged to the neck with Lottie's arms around me as I towed her around. Put her up on the jetty to a bayou cottage, watch her dry her naked body in the sun, my mark on her delicate skin as I paddled around like a total dick and showed off for her.

Brought her something fresh I killed for dinner. Loved her until she could barely keep her eyes open that night under a star-filled sky so bright she could read under its light if she chose, well away from civilization. Wake her every time she drifted off and love her some more with Gray.

Fuck, I needed her back so damn bad.

The player in me died the moment I set eyes on her.

"Fuck," Gray muttered, reappearing by my side. I zoned in my daydream. I hadn't realized he had left me alone in the entrance hall. "Eight missed calls." He listened to voicemail after voicemail, holding up a hand to silence me until he was done.

I shifted on my feet, too impatient, though my exhaustion slammed into me as I leaned against the wall.

Gray's frown annoyed me but he had plenty of energy. Lottie wore his mark and they bolstered each other regardless of the distance between them. I didn't have that luxury, wouldn't until she let me give her my mark.

If we ever fucking well found her again.

It was like finding her for the first time set off a ticking clock in me. Losing her already? It was a fast lane to a useless panther who couldn't protect the man I used to call brother, who had been my lover for the last years as we traveled together, pretending we weren't looking for the one impossible creature who evaded us as they did almost every panther shifter.

Our mate.

And now we had lost her.

"She's with the claw." Gray's crisp voice snapped me out of my daze. He flipped his phone over in his hand, a black rage suffusing his face.

"She ... why? What's she doing with them? Lottie isn't a shifter, is she?" I stared at him, rubbing a hand over my face as his blurred. *Wake the fuck up.* But I could barely stand. We'd run all day and my energy reserves were empty.

"Lionel took her. She was a test subject for the fucking drug of his. *Vapor.*" Gray sneered. The phone creaked in his hand. "Fuck. I should have asked more when I was there. I *knew* something wasn't right with him. That little weasel—no offense to weasel shifters—thought this was a good way to get one of us to breed with their females. They needed to find mates. Willing or unwilling, apparently it doesn't matter. He was worried about the breeding potential of the claw. Instead of building small family units like regular shifters, he intends to build a breeding *cell.*"

"Starting with Lottie." I pushed up off the wall, swaying where I stood.

"And us." Gray surveyed me with a closed expression I hated.

"Okay. Let's go." The world moved with me. My stomach rose to my throat.

Gray's hard expression softened. "Go to sleep,

Blake. I pushed you too hard."

"Shut up. She's my fucking mate too." I put a hand on the wall, missed the judgment of depth by a mile, and stumbled. "Fuck."

Gray caught me, his shoulder lodged beneath mine. "Stop, Blake," he murmured. "I'll get her, bring her home to you. You can give her your mark. Then we can all be together."

"Only if she wants it," I slurred as he guided me to the bed we had shared last night. "I won't force her."

His crooked smile left me warm as well as drowsy. "Sure thing. I'll just go get her, okay?" His mouth settled over mine in a gentle kiss, though after a moment his tongue swept along my bottom lip. I sighed and let him in, stroking his tongue with mine for a moment before he withdrew all too soon, though from the promise in his eyes I knew he wouldn't forget me.

"Come back, all right?" I whispered, exhaustion slamming into me as I dropped back onto the bed. My fingers flexed, needing to pull him closer, but I couldn't.

"Hell, no, I won't forget you." His hand squeezed my shoulder.

My eyes dropped shut, though not before I registered in some dim corner of my mind the concern etched across his carved face, and the determination there. I wondered if I would survive should Lottie refuse my mark again.

It will be worth it to see her face again.

I wondered if tonight I might lose them both when I couldn't be there to protect those I loved most. *Please, let them be safe.* My chest ached with love though as the world faded, so did the pain, and my fear.

And as I drifted into a sleep I wasn't sure I'd wake from, I wondered if any of it mattered at all.

Chapter Ten

Gray

Lionel stared at me over Lottie's purple-hazed eyes, his insane smile twisted with a dollop of cruelty. The latter came naturally to the ass-aholic leader of the NYC panther claw. The former? His insanity had better be temporary, or I'd find a way to remove that taint to his bloodline through a previously undiscovered orifice. Like his throat.

In fact, the only reason he still breathed was because of the three words he said that stopped me in my tracks a moment before. *"You were right."*

"I was what?" I didn't bother to keep my tone civilized. Or my claws—pun intended as it was the only sort I ever told—from sliding out where my nails should have been and raking them across the trash cans that lined the alley's depths.

Somewhere in the shadows, some poor shifter mewled. Retreating figures told me Lionel's strategy wasn't a popular choice. His champion wasn't anywhere in sight—probably locked in a breeding cage somewhere. His numbers depleted by the minute, even if he wasn't aware of that yet. What he did know was that he couldn't take me. Not alone.

Which was why he kept my mate held between us as a human shield.

That pithy offering wouldn't do shit for his fading mortality rate that reduced with every second he held a too-shiny motherfucking blade to my mate's throat. That plummeted further when the first bead of purple-tinged blood trickled across her alabaster skin.

How much of that shit did he pump into her?

"Repeat what you just said to me." I raked my claws across the brick of the nearest building.

Lionel winced and even Lottie, in her drug-fucked state, shuddered at the horrendous resulting sound.

"You were right." Lionel shrugged like my show ponying didn't bother him in the least.

I stared at the other shifter, not a hint of the shadows beneath his skin showing that should be there, or the claws he could shred Lottie's throat with...

The overwhelming scent hit me in a wave of arousal that hit me at a time I didn't want or need it, turning me worse than feral. *Pheromones.* Suddenly I knew what he was going to say before he said it.

"She was bait."

I stared back at him as full understanding dawned beyond the flurry of one-word text messages I exchanged with him back in the apartment. Acid rose from my belly in a reversal of gravity that changed my world and left my hands itching for the woman I'd lay my life down for.

"You heard me in the alley that night."

Lionel nodded. "I had to wait and see who claimed her. My choice wasn't popular with the claw, but then we don't have a lot of choices left. I think you've guessed."

"Your powers are weakened. You need her—*us*—to..." I canted my head, watching the powerless shifter lower his blade and counted the breaths out in my head. *Twenty. Nineteen. Eighteen...* "Breed?"

"New blood is needed. These walls are cages. They cripple us." He tapped the crumbling building at his side.

Sixteen. Fifteen.

A few extra shadows flitted backward leaving Lionel alone. Either he didn't notice, or he didn't care.

His self-imposed cafe had lost him that instinct too.

"You've done that to yourself." *Fourteen. Thirteen.* "Panthers should be wild. Free. This unnatural catastrophe … you're living the results."

He smiled at me sadly. "But if I set them free now, they'll die."

"That's already happening." The trail of purple blood stained Lottie's shirt, followed by a fresh trickle of red. The shadows writhed beneath my own skin, my exhausted beast writhing to the surface, ready to tear apart the pathetic creature who threatened our mate. "Give her to me."

Nine.

"And you'll let me go?" He laughed humorlessly.

"No," I said softly. "But I'll see my mate safe. My other mate needs her."

"You are the alpha." His sarcasm lacked pretty much anything.

I shot him a glance, reminded forcibly of Blake. I need to get back to him. More footsteps, this time slower, more curious ones, back toward us.

Four.

"I have my own to care for."

Three.

Lionel nodded, pushed Lottie forward.

Two.

She tottered toward me. I caught her as he spread his hands.

"Then do it."

One.

I held his gaze, shook my head. My arms tightened around her. No chance was I letting my mate go now she was exactly where she was supposed to be. *With me.*

"I don't need to," I said softly.

Gathering Lottie in my arms, I carried her from the alley unassailed as the first shifters used their remaining talents and tore into their leader who wore the brunt of their decisions.

For those ear-bleeding moments I was glad Lottie was too out of it to hear his screams.

****

Blake and Lottie lay side by side, pale as death in my bed as I covered them both in a nest of blankets and raised her wrist to his lips.

"Bite, brother. Mark her as ours," I whispered, pressing my lips to his temple.

Live. Please.

No matter how much he irritated the shit out of me, how many times I had to haul his ass out of trouble and across state and county lines … I still loved him. As much as I loved her.

"Did she agree?" he slurred. The tip of his tongue peeked between parched lips to taste her. A shudder rippled along his body at the mere scent of our mate, so close. But still he held back.

Lionel might have screwed his claw to the wall and worn the consequences, but I won't let Blake die because of some qualms when she's fucked out of her mind and it's not his fault.

Because she was in no state to say yes. So, I would say it for her.

"She agreed, Blake. She's yours," I lied, pressing her flesh to his lips.

"Finally," he mumbled around the too-thin limb, and bit.

His jaw was so fucking weak the mark didn't even take. Cursing low in my throat as his hands fell away, I slid in behind him, cupped my hands beneath his chin, and forced his bite.

A scream ripped from Lottie's throat as Blake's jaw locked around her wrist. He swallowed once, then again. Just as her eyes cleared, registering her pain—

So did his.

"You fucking asshole," he groused around her flesh.

Though he didn't let go of his prize, the cynical part of my possessive shifter-mind noted. I released his jaw and lay back, watching the show unfold before me.

Blake's energy unfolded in waves like the blankets he threw back as he arced over her, pushing her back. "I'm sorry, sweetness. But I need to have you now," he murmured. The tinge of regret in his eyes was fast hidden beneath a wave of molten desire even I could feel as he lifted her tiny form and pushed her between my spread legs.

Our mate panted, her head flicking back and forth as she took both of us in. Confusion scrolled across her face, though she seemed to be used to taking the strangeness of us in her stride by now.

"A few days with us, and we've altered your life." It was as close an apology as she'd get from me.

Asshole that might make me, but the way she looked at me, all wide eyes without a hint of that godforsaken purple haze thankfully inhabiting her gaze, she was the most tempting damn creature I'd ever seen. Right now, that honor belonged to someone else.

Blake gripped my thigh in warning as he positioned her as he wanted. Offering him a slow nod I closed my hands around Lottie's hips, dragging her up my body until her back pressed to my chest. Her sweet struggles, not really a fight after all, more a squirm of anticipation as she studied the bite on her wrist and the shifter who marked her, rubbed her warmth between us.

"Shall I?" I offered, raking my claw tips lightly across her body.

Blake nodded tersely. Pupils blown wide, his gaze coasted over her form as he mouthed words neither of us could hear but we both understood with perfect clarity.

I'm sorry I'm sorry I'm sorry—

"It's all right. I wanted you to." Lottie's forgiveness blazed from her like a beacon, calling to him. To us.

I wrapped my arms tight around her knowing she'd need the support in a moment as he shucked his jeans to his knees, pushed her flimsy dress aside. Both of us hooked a claw in her panties, and I raised my hand, half transformed across her stretched out, vulnerable body like the perfect offering.

"Stay still, sweet thing," I murmured against her ear. My tongue darted out to taste the shell.

Then I swiped my fully extended claws across her softness as Blake flicked his wrist.

Every inch of material shredded from her lithe body.

"Too beautiful," Blake murmured reverently, leaning down to press his lips to the mark he gave her, licking and sucking as she moaned for him, whispered his name. His gaze darted up to mine.

I swallowed hard, tilting her head to the side, asking an unspoken question of my own.

Are you sure?

Blake nodded. Just once.

Breathing out a long exhale I licked Lottie's neck gently, then clamped my mouth over my own mark, its permanent shadows dark and angry against her pale flesh, sucking hard. Blake mirrored me, laving and sucking at her wrist until she arched between us.

I slid fully beneath her body, shoving my jeans down. "Be fast, Blake. Or you'll lose your turn."

His smile when he raised his head was nothing short of feral. "Together."

A growl of agreement reverberated in my chest as I dropped a hand between her legs to find his cock where he rubbed against her and worked him hard. *It's been too long.* "Together, then."

Blake moaned and surged into my hand until our balls nestled together in the sticky warmth of her thighs. "Fuck, too good. Make me paint her first," he begged me.

My grip tightened. "That's how you want to claim your mate? Scent her skin like a feral dog?" I snarled, working him faster.

Fuck, I wish I'd thought of that first. The thought turned me on until I wondered if I'd join him and coat her back in my cum before either of us sank into her heat.

"Don't I get a choice in this?" Lottie panted between us. Her hands wandered freely across Blake's chest and shoulders, touching him as he had never permitted her contact before she allowed his mark once I fucked her. Out of self-preservation, I suspected.

Or forgave him for taking it.

"Not tonight, Lottie," I murmured. Pumping Blake's cock faster in a painfully inescapable grip, I jerked him over her stomach as I held myself still beneath them both. "Watch him spend himself for you. Only for you."

Lottie's giggle froze us both.

She tipped her head back, looking at me upside down. *And she's still so fucking cute.* "No, silly. He's coming for you, too."

Blake groaned, surging into my hand to prove her point on cue as he leaned down to kiss her upside-down mouth gently, then transferred her taste to my lips. His tongue slid inside as his warm seed soaked my fingers and her stomach. I let him take control if only for a moment, offering his thanks. Blake's kisses were liquid heat, and I knew from experience he was far from done. We would be fucking our girl for hours, long after she was through with us.

He licked my lips clean of his kiss. "Thank you," Blake murmured, holding my gaze. "For everything."

I pressed my forehead to his. "You're welcome."

Warm heat squirmed between our taut bodies, reminding me of the third amongst us.

"Not that I object to seeing the two of you go at it, but can I join in?"

I stared down into Lottie's luminous, haze-free eyes, and my cock surged with fresh blood.

Chapter Eleven

Lottie

The moment Gray registered my need, I knew I was in trouble.

His eyes flared the color of his name, and the hand holding Blake's not-so-soft cock flattened over the mess they left of my stomach. Gray rubbed the cum into my skin thoughtfully.

"Have you had two men at once, sweet thing?" His voice came out all raspy and thick as I arched back, tipping my mouth up as I sought his.

A groan left his chest, the sound rumbling beneath me that grew as his mouth connected with mine in a harsh, desperate kiss until a third tongue slithered in. Blake's liquid heat softened Gray's harsher edge, though he added a heady tang to my desperation. I linked my legs around his waist, covering us both in his earlier release, though he didn't seem to care.

"No," I whispered back when Gray broke away, swearing softly. "I've only had one..." I cleared my throat as my cheeks heated. "One partner before you."

Man didn't seem appropriate when dark shadows roiled beneath Gray's skin, his claw-tipped hands digging into my hips while Blake's eyes fluctuated the sort of green I'd previously only ever associated with the hues of a jungle after rain that I'd seen on TV.

"Tonight we will stretch you," Blake murmured against my mouth. "You'll take both your mates and pleasure us both. Won't you?" His malachite gaze shot with amazonian lime locked onto me.

"Yes," I managed, leaning back and letting Gray

take my weight without fighting him any longer.

The soft rumble in his chest changed to a sound of approval, like a faint summer storm, as Blake notched his cock, thick and hard at my entrance. No, not just himself, *both* of them.

"I'm not ready—" I objected. Or at least I started to object, but Gray's claws slipped over my stomach.

Glided lower.

Fear gilded my veins.

"No—" I gasped.

But the slicked finger pads that stroked my clit were soft, if calloused.

"Come for us, pet," Gray murmured, easing my head back onto his shoulder as he played my body to his rhythm. "Make this nice and slick and easy for all of us."

I whimpered as bliss edged around my consciousness, the haze so similar to the drug collapsing my reality if only for a second. "Please kiss me," I begged.

Gray's groan burst across my lips as he savaged them. His eyes became my world as I screamed his name if only in my head, though I got the impression he heard me anyway. My thighs quaked when I blinked again. Even though my orgasm had long crested the power of having them both together, wearing their marks, seemed to prolong the aftereffects.

Blake cradled my hips gently as he rubbed their thick cocks against my entrance. "So nice and hot and wet, sweetness. Gonna be good and give me one of those screams now?"

Heat suffused my cheeks. Maybe my neck and my breasts too. "I didn't think you heard."

"Oh, we both heard, pet. Loud and fucking clear. I nearly came on command for you." Gray nuzzled my neck and sucked on his mark until I moaned. "Do it again?"

"Me first." Blake wasted no more time, pushing both of them into me. *Inside me.*

My mouth opened to do as they bid quite willingly, but no sound came out. I wasn't sure *breath* came out.

Blake paused halfway, arched over me, his hands braced with Gray's on my hips. Pinpoints of claws dug into my skin but I welcomed the pain against the onslaught of excess stimulation as my mind went into overdrive.

"Like that," Gray nuzzled me again. "*Mate.*"

He shifted beneath me, and together they surged forward, filling me.

I swore my body split open in place, or maybe my mind did. Heat seared my insides as they thrust together, bottoming out somewhere deeper than I'd ever been touched. Their spines opened, grazing my insides delicately.

Groans left them both as their cocks rubbed together and I realized how torturous and pleasurable this was for both of them as it was for me. More than in a physical sense, they fucked me together. All three of us, linked by a tangle of limbs and gasping mouths, slicked secret places only those connected at a soul-etched level could reach.

Blake panted above me as I curled forward and screamed into his shoulder, my lips forming his name as I promised. "Sweetness, you keep coming on our cocks like that and you're gonna find yourself sleep-deprived real damn fast."

"But also loved. And worshipped." Gray nipped at my neck lightly, then licked where he hurt me.

I mewled at the strange touch, rolling my hips as my pussy contracted on them both. And both of them groaned for me.

A wicked thought brushed my mind, and I squeezed them both again, hard.

"Pet..." Gray's claws dug into my hip, deeper than just the tips this time.

"Yes, Gray?" I whispered innocently.

He drove his hips upward at a brutal pace until I screamed his name, begging—for breath, sanity, *more*—then Blake joined him and my world...

Well, it grayed out too.

And when I pried my eyes open, all I saw was charcoal tinged with a hint of jungle green before lids dropped shut.

"Sleep, sweetness." Blake kissed me until I wasn't sure if I kissed him back, or dreamt it.

I fell asleep to the rhythm of his thrusts inside me, or maybe Gray's. They had promised me they'd go all night. I just hadn't considered I'd need to be awake for their nocturnal activities.

Sweetly welcomed bliss washed over me, and I let them play.

Chapter Twelve

Blake

Our mate liked to watch.

She also loved to swim and couldn't cook, not that I gave two fucks about that last.

We left New York in a hurry. Well, the next sunrise Lottie could walk on after we fucked her and ourselves into oblivion. Not that we made her walk—at least, not all the way to Bartholomew Bayou where we spent the last of my money, Mister Tight-ass never being willing to part with his own—on a double-story stilted cottage in Arkansas.

I winced when Gray announced his grand plan, certain Lottie was about to teach him what a fist to the face finally felt like. Hell, did I earn a sunrise surprise when she jumped him and they screwed like bunnies all over the apartment that morning. Left to my own devices, I looked up a stack of places, found the one I liked best, and threw a deposit on it before Gray was any the wiser.

That earned *me* a heady kiss and a dozen hours on my knees as recompense … which was how we found out our mate liked to watch. Once we arrived, unpacked our meager belongings, we discovered Lottie liked to lie on her back in the sun with my head between her legs, and my knees developing new calluses while Gray held my literal balls in his hand and ploughed my asshole purely for her entertainment. And maybe for his, too.

Mind, she came on my tongue so beautifully, I barely minded not being able to walk for at least two reasons the next day.

Lottie's hands tangled freely in my hair urging me deeper as water lapped around the cottage's stilts. I speared my tongue into her delicious pussy, groaning as her slick walls flushed with a fresh round of heat and cream for me.

"Fuck, you're delicious," I muttered, lapping at her.

"Feels good," she moaned back, rocking into me.

"Shut up and remember why you're our bitch for the month," Gray snarled, gripping my balls in one fist and pulling my sack tight.

I groaned as he pulsed his fingers rhythmically, enough for me to want to burst at the seams while he buried his thick-spined shaft deep in my ass, torturing me, but his grip was tight enough to prevent me from spending just yet.

A quick glance between my legs proved my cockhead was as angry and red-colored as my back and ass probably were—from the heat and sun, not from Gray's spanks, though he wasn't shy on that front.

"Don't our girl deserve your dick?" I groused, laving her clit gently.

"Yes please," she murmured.

"Not today, pet." Gray leaned over me, burying himself deeper than ever in my bowels, and kissed her as he jacked his hips painfully just to prove his point. His spines flared, lodging in place, raking my walls. "But if you roll over, I think your boy wants to fill that pretty cunt with his seed. Could you do that?" he muttered mockingly into my ear, biting the lobe as he jerked on my ball sack.

"Yes, please, Gray," I gasped, rutting at him as I fucked myself on his cock, wearing his pain.

"Good little slut, isn't he?" Gray laughed as Lottie positioned herself beneath me and worked my straining, painful cock that needed to come so badly into her sopping, freshly licked cunt. "Why don't you spread those lovely legs, pet, and let him rut his slutty need out for us both, hmm?"

"Will you do that?" she asked softly, seeking my consent as she looked over her shoulder at me with wide eyes.

Her pretty little pussy I'd spent an hour kissing hugged my cock to perfection.

"Anything for you, sweetness," I mumbled back. "Don't you fucking let go," I warned Gray.

His laugh echoed across the deceptively still waters. "You'll regret saying that when your asshole is gaping later."

"It'll be worth it."

At least the local gator shifter population would get a good show. Fuck knew what they thought of us, but they seemed to understand we came out here to hide from the world and they left us well enough alone in the interim. We would see how long that fragile peace lasted.

"Hold me tight," I whispered.

Gray heard, and strangled my balls until I swore they turned blue.

Then I did as he asked so nicely, and humiliated myself for them both, fucking myself raw between his cock and her soaked, welcoming hole until they both shuddered around me. Only when Gray's weight bore me into the boards and my arms trembled, unable to sustain both our weight any longer, did he let go of my balls.

I knew he'd let me ruin but Lottie helped, massaging and milking my cock with her hot little pussy I spent so long worshipping, until I came with a strangled scream. Gray swallowed my sounds as he tongued my mouth lewdly, a show for her as I flooded her cunt and thighs with my need for the mate we found abandoned in an alley one night beneath a feral moon rising.

The End

VOLUME FOUR

EVERNIGHT PUBLISHING ®

www.evernightpublishing.com